A Noise Interrupted
Her Restless Dreaming...

"Who's there?" Roberta asked sharply. "Don't come any nearer, for I'm holding a loaded pistol."

There was no answer.

"If you think to harm me, it would be a mistake," she said quickly, "for I only have to shout and my maid will be here in a trice."

She found the continuing silence unnerving and her earlier bravado evaporated. She made her way slowly over to the dresser. Suddenly a hand caught her right ankle in a viselike grip.

"My dear lady," a man said, "what I would like to know is what you are doing in my room."

Dear Reader:

We've had thousands of wonderful surprises at SECOND CHANCE AT LOVE since we launched the line in June 1981.

We knew we were going to have to work hard to bring you the six best romances we could each month. We knew we were working with a talented, caring group of authors. But we *didn't* know we were going to receive such a warm and generous response from readers. So the thousands of wonderful surprises are in the form of letters from readers like you who've been kind with your praise, constructive and helpful with your suggestions. We read each letter...and take it seriously.

It's been a thrill to "meet" our readers, to discover that the people who read SECOND CHANCE AT LOVE novels and write to us about them are so remarkable. Our romances can only get better and better as we learn more and more about you, the reader, and what you like to read.

So, I hope you will continue to enjoy SECOND CHANCE AT LOVE and, if you haven't written to us before, please feel free to do so. If you have written, keep in touch.

With every good wish,

Sincerely,

Carolyn Nichols

Carolyn Nichols
SECOND CHANCE AT LOVE
The Berkley/Jove Publishing Group
200 Madison Avenue
New York, New York 10016

P.S. Because your opinions *are* so important to us, I urge you to fill out and return the questionnaire in the back of this book.

Second Chance at Love

REGENCY

INTRIGUING LADY
DAPHNE WOODWARD

A SECOND CHANCE AT LOVE BOOK

INTRIGUING LADY

First edition published April 1982

First printing

"Second Chance at Love" and the butterfly emblem are trademarks belonging to Jove Publications, Inc.

Printed in the United States of America

Second Chance at Love books are published by
The Berkley/Jove Publishing Group,
200 Madison Avenue, New York, NY 10016

For

> Nancy with the sparkling eyes
> and
> Louise, who was so generous with
> her time

chapter 1

THE OLD-FASHIONED traveling carriage which was carrying Miss Roberta Rushforth and her companion, Mrs. Ashley, on the final stage of their journey across France toward England moved at a fast pace. The speed was dictated by Roberta, who, after six months' absence from her native land, was anxious to return.

Williams, the coachman, a wiry old gent, clucked his disapproval of the pace every time he urged the horses on; yet, having known his mistress from the hour she entered the world some seven and twenty years ago, he suspected she would take over the reins if he ignored her orders.

"It comes to summat that we've got to risk breaking our necks to get back in time to see the bloomin' flowers," he muttered in the northern brogue that he stubbornly retained even though he had lived most of his adult life in London. "I've never 'eard of such nonsense in me life."

His indignation was caused not only by the speed but by the fact that the party presented an undignified appearance as the horses dashed pell-mell along the bumpy, ill-kept roads. Moreover, since leaving Switzerland, he had not been treated with the respect he had come to regard as his right, and even taking into consideration the outmoded traveling conveyance, it was hard for him to conceive that no one in France had ever heard of the Rushforth family or was willing to pay homage to that old, illustrious name. From the moment they had left Switzerland, he had had a constant fight to get decent accommodations for his mistress, and on at least three occasions, he himself had been forced to sleep over the stables.

"Not tonight, though," he told himself grimly, "for no matter what 'er ladyship says, we're going no farther than Le Cateau. Henri will be only too willing to see that we're treated in the proper manner." Henri Lamonte was his late wife's cousin and had inherited Le Cheval Blanc, the only hostelry Le Cateau sported.

The two occupants sat gazing at the passing scenery from their respective windows, oblivious to the coachman's misery. Mrs. Ashley's hands were busy with her tatting, while Roberta's elegantly gloved ones were impatiently drumming on the faded upholstery.

The dramatic scenery of Switzerland had long since been replaced by the dull, rolling countryside of France, and this didn't suit Roberta's mood at all. Their journey thus far had been uneventful, unless one were to count as exciting one of the horses going lame just outside Metz.

Now, with nothing more to do than sit in the carriage, with only Mrs. Ashley for company, Roberta was bored.

She was finally roused from her brown study when she realized that Williams was slowing the coach. "I wonder if there has been an accident," she remarked, her melodious voice breaking the silence that had prevailed all morning. But the pause was only fleeting, and they soon resumed the earlier fast pace. "Poor Williams," she continued, covering behind a determined smile her disappointment that there was to be no diversion. "He must be rueing the day he ever sought service with the Rushforths. I think these past two weeks have been a sore trial to his dignity."

"As they have been to mine, Roberta," Mrs. Ashley rejoined as she tried, unsuccessfully, to resettle her large frame more comfortably. "But then, you were ever the one to set your own pace. And once you've got an idea fixed in your mind, there's no stopping you. I just hope we reach London in one piece."

Mrs. Ashley spoke with the ease of an old retainer, which she was. For when Roberta had been orphaned at the age of five, Lord Bromley, Roberta's uncle and guardian, had hired Mrs. Ashley with explicit instructions to provide Roberta with love and affection, which hadn't proved the least bit difficult. The child had been an engaging little soul, even though she tended toward wildness at times.

As Roberta had grown older, this wildness had turned into a savage independence. This, in Mrs. Ashley's considered opinion, had ultimately cooled the ardor of her many suitors when she had made her debut seven years ago. Even so, it still was a puzzlement to Mrs. Ashley that, with her looks, breeding and fortune, Roberta hadn't been snapped up by some worthy gentleman willing to overlook this flaw in her character. There had been one, but he had been altogether unsuitable, and Mrs. Ashley could only hope that Roberta had forgotten him.

Now Mrs. Ashley wondered what the future held for her charge and worried lest, on their return, Roberta would be dubbed an old maid by the people who knew her best. She turned her gaze inward and studied her charge intently, looking for any overt signs of the miracle that had so recently occurred. There were none, despite the tedium of the journey. She still looked pale, which accentuated her brown-flecked hazel eyes. But the thinness of her figure was carefully disguised by an elegant and obviously expensive emerald gown, and her flaming red hair, cut in an unfashionably short bob, was hidden beneath a wide-brimmed bonnet.

"I do wish Dr. Steinway hadn't insisted on cutting your hair so short," Mrs. Ashley said, shaking her head in regret. "It will take forever to grow back to its original length."

Roberta laughed at Mrs. Ashley's melancholy expression and reached over to squeeze her hand. "I thought to keep it like this," she teased, "for I find it prodigiously easy to take care of."

"Roberta!" Mrs. Ashley exclaimed in shocked tones. "Don't even jest about such a thing. I cannot think that you will enjoy being seen abroad, sporting such an unfashionable frizz. Why, people will think you an eccentric." She shuddered at the thought. "No, no, my dear. Now that you are cured, there is no need at all to worry that growing it long will sap your strength. No need at all."

Roberta appeared to consider this for a while and then relented as she saw the look of worry in Mrs. Ashley's eyes.

"Well," she said, "if it makes you feel easier, I will agree to do as you wish. Anyway, it's fashionable for a female of my advanced years to hide her burnished glory beneath a cap."

Mrs. Ashley smiled her acceptance of this compromise but ignored the last piece of bamming.

"I hope you are not concerned that your condition will recur, Roberta," she remarked. "Dr. Steinway was most emphatic that your lungs are completely clear."

"That is the least of my worries." Roberta laughed. "Having just spent the last six months undergoing what I can only consider to be the most grueling of treatments, I have no intention of ever being sick again in my life. Oh, Ashley!" she continued, her boredom forgotten for the moment, "it's a wonderfully exhilarating thought to know that I have been cured. Do you remember when we thought I'd never breathe properly again? And the time I was convinced I'd never see another English spring? You spent the best part of a week persuading me otherwise. What nonsense I must have spoken, yet never once did you withdraw your support."

She broke off as the carriage came to a halt. Looking out the window, she noticed they were standing in the middle of a cobblestoned courtyard. "What is it, Williams?" she asked as she opened the window.

Williams clambered down from his perch and made his way slowly around the carriage. He opened the door and lowered the steps with a flourish. "Nothing's amiss," he muttered. "I just thought as 'ow you might like to spend a night in a comfortable bed, for a change, and partake of the excellent food for which this inn is renowned."

"We're not stopping!" Roberta exclaimed. She could now see the inn. It was a pretty, white-stoned, gabled building covered in a flowering creeper. She felt instinctively it would be a pleasant place to spend the night. Yet she continued perversely, "Why, there must still be two hours of daylight left."

"If you will pardon me for saying so, Miss Roberta, I've 'ad about as much as I can take for one day. This dampness 'as gotten into my joints summat awful, and I can 'ardly move my right 'and."

"Oh, Williams, you poor man!" Impetuously, Roberta

jumped to the ground and took the aging servant by the arm. "I insist that we stay here until you feel better, even if it means a delay of a week."

Her concern was genuine, until the landlord appeared from a side door. As he hurried over, he greeted Williams as a long-lost friend. Roberta drew back and in severe tones ordered Williams to her side. "Is this some ploy you've thought up to spend some time dallying with an old acquaintance?" she demanded. "Where are we?"

Williams shuffled from one foot to the other and resolutely refused to look up at Roberta's severe countenance. "We're but two days from Calais, Miss Roberta," he wheedled, "and I thought to myself as 'ow you wouldn't mind putting up at 'Enri's inn."

Henri began to shake his head. "*Mon dieu*, but it is *impossible*. I have rooms, yes, but not one available that is suitable for a lady. It . . . it is *impossible. Impossible.*"

Roberta eyed the rotund little Frenchman for a moment. He threw his hands in the air in a gesture of finality. There was something in his manner that aroused her curiosity. She gave him a haughty stare and then turned to Williams. "You may tell him, Williams, that I am too tired to travel farther today, and that I will take whatever rooms he has."

"*C'est très difficile,*" Henri muttered without waiting for the message to be relayed. "The English lord has bespoke my best rooms and . . . and . . . *non, mademoiselle,* I think it not a good thing for you to inconvenience yourself by staying here."

"I don't know what's gotten into 'im, Miss Roberta," Williams declared angrily. "And we're supposed to be related. Now, look 'ere, Henri," he continued, "you 'eard what Miss Rushforth said. We'll take whatever rooms you 'ave, and be done with it. It's just not dignified for you to behave in such a fashion, and 'ere's me thinking as 'ow you'd be pleased to see me after all these years."

Henri hastened to apologize, but Williams, his pride wounded, refused to listen. Instead, he turned back to the carriage and inquired of Mrs. Ashley whether she was ready to descend.

Meanwhile, Roberta, sorry that she had caused a rift between the two men, hastened to put Henri at ease. "Williams will come about, for he seldom takes offense and never holds a grudge," she said in reassuring tones. "So please do not dwell on what he just said. Perhaps your wife could show me to my rooms?"

Henri shook his head unhappily. "Mademoiselle . . ." he began, and then, catching sight of Williams's outraged face, continued in more accommodating tones, "I will see what can be arranged for your comfort. Please, this way."

Roberta, her curiosity now fully roused, nodded and, without waiting for Mrs. Ashley, followed Henri through the front door. The hallway was gleaming. The flagstone floor, dotted with rush mats, looked as though it had only just been scrubbed, and the walls were covered with an assortment of horse brasses, pen-and-ink sketches and brass rubbings.

"Please . . . please excuse me," Henri said. "I will go fetch my wife." He bowed low and left the room hurriedly.

Roberta could hear voices raised in argument, although the actual conversation was indistinct. Finally, there was a silence, and then the door opened and a pleasant-faced, middle-aged woman entered.

"Mademoiselle Rushforth, I'm Marie, Henri's wife. I beg you to excuse his bad manners. You must, of course, have our best rooms, and I have sent the chambermaid up to prepare them for you. Perhaps, while you wait, you would care for something to drink?"

Roberta nodded. "You are too kind, Marie. I have no desire to cause your other guest offense, though. The rooms you have available will be perfectly all right, I'm sure."

"Non, non, mademoiselle. They are over the taproom, and sometimes the noise can be quite horrendous. You know how men get when they have had a few brandies."

Roberta had heard enough stories from her uncle about the raucous behavior of some of his bibulous friends to enable her now to nod and smile knowingly. "I can only hope the Englishman will not mind," she said.

"Oh, I doubt he will be here tonight. He had business in another village and is not expected back until morning. So you see, it is quite a simple matter to rearrange things to accommodate you. But Henri, his mind is not so flexible." She threw her hands in the air to express her exasperation and left Roberta, promising to bring in some refreshments immediately.

Roberta looked about her and liked what she saw. The ceiling was low and beamed, and the deep-set windows overlooked a rose garden. Floral curtains were held back by red braids, and the cushions on the country-style chairs and sofa were covered in a matching fabric.

"Charming," she murmured as she moved to inspect the stone fireplace. "Absolutely charming."

"Isn't it just?" Mrs. Ashley concurred as she entered. "I'm so pleased Williams stopped here, for I can confess now that a break in our journey is what I need."

"Why don't we stop here for a few days, then?" Roberta suggested impulsively. "If the weather brightens, we might even explore the countryside."

"An excellent idea, Roberta," Mrs. Ashley said. "I think a little bit of peace and quiet is the best thing for us."

"And maybe," Roberta mused, "I can discover why Henri seemed so reluctant to let us stay here in the first place." A mischievous smile lit her face. "If there is a mystery to be solved, it would certainly break the tedium we have suffered so far."

"Now, now, Roberta, there is no need to be looking for trouble. Just content yourself with partaking of some walks and putting some color into your cheeks. I want you to look healthy when we arrive in England."

"Yes, Ashley, of course," Roberta responded meekly. "Why don't you tell Henri of our change in plan, while I go and inspect the garden."

She left the room before Mrs. Ashley could reply. She had seen a young boy bearing a striking resemblance to their host, just outside the windows, and she wanted to have a word with him before he disappeared. Perhaps he could provide a few of the answers she sought.

When she reentered the inn some fifteen minutes later, there was a satisfied expression on her face. Jacques, for that had been the lad's name, had been most helpful. She had learned that the absent Englishman's business involved a local beauty with whom he was passionately in love. She couldn't help but be intrigued.

chapter 2

THE NIGHT WAS well advanced when Roberta finally readied herself for bed. She had spent a pleasant evening with Mrs. Ashley in their private sitting room, making plans for her reemergence into Society. But alone now, memories she had thought long-suppressed came flooding back, keeping her awake.

The face of Stephen Davenport danced in front of her eyes. She cradled her head in her hands and wished, without any real hope, for a miracle that would dull the pain she felt every time she thought of him. Eighteen months had elapsed since she had sent Stephen away forever, yet she knew without a doubt she still loved him.

She sighed in defeat as she sat in front of her dresser, enveloped in a brooding silence. She realized that, for tonight, at least, it was a useless fight to keep her memories of Stephen at bay. Stephen was the man she was to have married, despite the disapproval shown by her guardian, Lord Bromley, and by Mrs. Ashley. She had ignored their advice not to encourage his suit, for her love of him had been overwhelming, and she hadn't been able to envisage life without him.

He was not overly tall, yet in his presence she felt dwarfed. His physique was truly masculine: broad shoulders, narrow waist and slender hips. His style was unmistakably Corinthian, whether he was dressed in his finest velvets and satins or the buckskin pantaloons and tailored jackets made for him by Weston.

They had met at Lady Chandler's rout two years ago, and been drawn to each other instantly. After she had stood up with him three times that first evening, all the matrons had nodded knowingly. His background was hazy, though, and this had been the cause of Lord Bromley's disapproval. Many of Roberta's acquaintances had tried to convince her that he was no more than a fortune hunter, but privately he had told her he had great expectations of inheriting his maternal uncle's large estate in Scotland. He never pretended to be anything more than the youngest son of an impoverished earl, and she saw no reason to press him for additional information. Mrs. Ashley thought him evasive about the source of his income, but Roberta retorted that it was not her business to pry.

When he proposed, she had accepted instantly, although at her urging they kept the engagement secret. She had hoped to persuade Lord Bromley to accept Stephen before any public announcement was made, for she was extremely fond of her uncle and wanted to avoid angering him.

It was at this point that she succumbed to the ailment. At first she had refused to believe it was a serious condition, but by the time she had consulted four different specialists, she was convinced she was suffering from something worse than mere inflammation of the lungs. And immediately upon learning that her chances of making a full recovery were almost nonexistent, she decided to free Stephen from the engagement. She thought she understood him well enough to know he would, in the long run, resent being shackled to a semi-invalid.

She used her uncle's disapproval as the reason for sending him away. He refused to believe her at first, but when she insisted, and he could see she would not change her mind, he left her, vowing he would marry the first woman he met. And he did—Lady Anita Edwards, a widow of independent means.

Unfortunately, this event only served to convince her uncle that his original summation of Stephen's character had been correct, and his castigation of Stephen had been lengthy and virulent. However, as Roberta was convinced she had acted in Stephen's best interests, she remained silent, even though she knew she was serving him a shabby trick by letting her uncle and Mrs. Ashley believe the worst of him. Her great fear that Stephen would insist on standing by her if he should ever discover the truth hadn't diminished until he had married his widow. And by then, she reasoned, to reveal the truth wouldn't serve any useful purpose.

"If only I had heard of Dr. Steinway and his cure earlier, all this misery would have been averted." She sighed unhappily, picked up her brush and idly began to brush her hair. "What good does it do me to dwell on what has passed?" she asked her image. "Am I to spend the rest of my life in regret?" She shook her head firmly. "No! Marriage without love is something I do not seek, but I am certainly of an age whereby I can enjoy myself." Suddenly filled with determination to live to the full, she climbed into bed and blew out the candles. Within minutes she drifted off to sleep.

When a noise interrupted her restless dreaming, she immediately thought it came from the taproom. She sat up in bed, annoyed that she had been awakened, and as she did so she heard a thud, this time near at hand. Peering into the darkness, she thought she saw something move by the windows, but then chided herself for letting her imagination run wild. She was sure she had closed the shutters.

By now, she was fully awake, and she decided to investigate just in case one of the cats had found its way into her room. As she reached over to relight the candles, a barely audible moan broke the silence.

"Who's there?" she asked sharply. "Don't come any nearer, for I'm holding a loaded pistol."

There was no answer.

Alarmed now, she inched her way out of bed and grasped the brass candlestick firmly in her right hand. If anyone attacked her, she was certainly going to put up a fight.

"If you want my jewels," she continued in a steady voice, "I'm afraid I don't have them with me, and—and my money is hidden in my coach."

Another moan greeted this piece of information. It sounded as though it came from near the dresser. Whoever was in her room had managed to crawl almost to the door.

"If you think to harm me, it would be a mistake," she said quickly, "for I only have to shout and my maid will be here in a trice." She found the continuing silence unnerving, and her earlier bravado evaporated. She made her way slowly over to the dresser, feeling her way carefully in the darkness. She had almost reached it when she heard a noise to her left. She whirled around, but before she could move, a hand caught her right ankle in a viselike grip. She let out a strangled scream and tried to kick free.

"My dear lady," a man said, "what I would like to know is what you are doing in my room."

Her fears evaporated, for to her ear the voice was not only English but extremely cultured. Somehow, she couldn't bring herself to believe that a fellow countryman would cause her harm. She was about to inquire who he was, when he moaned again. His grip went slack, and suddenly her ankle was free.

"Are you all right?" she asked in alarm, fearful lest he had suffered a fatal injury. No matter what his reasons for being in her room, she certainly didn't wish that fate for him.

She fumbled on the dresser until her fingers located the flint, and quickly lit the candles. Holding the light aloft, she looked down.

"Good heavens above!" she gasped. The man, quite obviously of the first stare, lay at her feet. His dull copper hair was swept back off his face in a style Roberta didn't recognize, and his harsh features were accentuated by his pallor. His mouth was firm, and his chin jutted out arrogantly. His age was difficult to determine in the flickering light, but if she had to hazard a guess, she would have said that he had seen his thirtieth birthday a few years back.

She knelt down and looked at him more closely. He appeared to be in a dead faint, and blood was seeping from a wound in his arm, an ever-widening stain coating his pale-gold satin jacket. His breathing was shallow but regular.

"I wonder what this is all about?" she murmured as she arose. "I had better fetch Henri immediately."

She placed the candlestick on the dresser and hurried over to her silken negligee. Pulling it on with trembling hands, she tied the ribbons with difficulty. Then, gathering up her cotton petticoats, she ran to the door, opened it and stepped into the corridor. She glanced up and down, hoping to see someone who could help. Nobody was about. Without hesitation, she rapped on Mrs. Ashley's door and called out urgently.

"Ashley, Ashley! Quickly! Come to my room immediately!"

She flew back to her room and, seeing that the gentleman was still prone, knelt down beside him again and began to rip up her petticoats. She had just finished fashioning a tourniquet when Mrs. Ashley appeared. Without looking up, Roberta commanded her to fetch Henri.

"And leave you alone with a man?" Mrs. Ashley asked in strangled tones. She was truly shocked by the sight that confronted her, yet all she could whisper was, "Have . . . have you killed him?"

"Lordy me, no, Ashley! Please just do as I ask. Fetch Henri immediately, and for goodness' sake don't make a fuss." She continued to apply the makeshift bandage to the gentleman's arm as she spoke.

"This—this is an absolute outrage," Mrs. Ashley said, stubbornly refusing to leave. "Who is he? How did he get into your room? I'll have a word with Williams in the morning and tell him exactly what I think of his cousin's inn."

"Please, Ashley," Roberta interrupted, knowing that if she allowed the woman to continue, there would be no stopping her. "There isn't time for you to enact a full-length Cheltenham tragedy. Fetch Henri and tell him there is an injured man here."

Mrs. Ashley turned and left, only to reappear a few minutes later with Henri in tow. "I met him on the stairs," she informed Roberta in frigid tones. "Now, Roberta, would you mind leaving the—the man and coming with me? I— I don't know what your uncle would say if he should ever hear of this."

Roberta stood up, satisfied that she had stemmed the flow of blood, and ignored Mrs. Ashley. She turned to Henri.

"I take it this is the English lord you were speaking of earlier?"

"Roberta!" Mrs. Ashley interjected. "Come to my room immediately."

"Please, Ashley, don't fuss. I want to get to the bottom of this. Am I correct, Henri?"

Henri nodded, the embarrassment he felt obvious and acute.

"Would you mind giving me an explanation?" Roberta asked in deceptively mild tones. "After all, I do think I'm owed one, don't you?"

"If you had only listened to me, mademoiselle, when you had first arrived, this—this wouldn't have happened," Henri protested as he edged his way over to the Englishman. He knelt down and felt for a pulse.

"He's all right, I think," Roberta said, suddenly amused by the man's rudeness. "But perhaps we should carry him to my bed and call for a doctor."

"Non, non. That will not be necessary. I will myself take a look at the wound. First, if you wouldn't mind, I will fetch my son. He can help me."

As Henri left, Mrs. Ashley rounded on Roberta. "Really, Roberta, I would never have believed you could behave in such a vulgar fashion. I—I—"

"For goodness' sake, Ashley, where's your sense of adventure?" Roberta asked. "We have a real mystery to unravel, and all you can concern yourself with is proprieties. Where is your compassion for a fellow countryman? Do you propose we abandon him to his fate in a foreign country? Oh, Ashley! Don't you see, he may need our help."

"It appears to me, Roberta, that Henri has everything well in hand. I do not see the necessity of involving ourselves in the affair."

"Dear Ashley," Roberta cajoled, her eyes brimming with excitement, "please don't overset yourself. Let me find out what this is all about, and then I'll do as you wish. Don't you see, when I return to England, I'll have no choice but to conform to the dreadful rules Society dictates."

Before Mrs. Ashley could reply, Henri and his son, Jacques, returned. She watched in silence as the two men lifted the Englishman up and laid him gently on the bed.

"Go to His Lordship's room, Jacques, and bring back a nightshirt," Henri commanded in a low voice. "Then we can undress him and make him comfortable."

"Who is he, Henri?" Roberta asked impatiently. "I think it time you explained what is happening."

"I don't know that it is my business to tell you, mademoiselle," Henri began. "It's not the wish of His Lordship to have his name known, I think."

"Come, Henri," Roberta responded in exasperation. "You may as well tell me, for I will refuse to leave until I have the answer."

"But mademoiselle . . ."

The Englishman, forgotten for a moment by Roberta and Henri as they argued, shifted uncomfortably on the bed, and his eyes flickered open. Roberta, unaware that she was being observed, stared haughtily down at Henri and in lofty tones informed him that she did not intend to spend the rest of the night bandying words with an innkeeper.

A roguish smile touched the edges of the Englishman's firm mouth until he was overcome by a fit of coughing.

Roberta spun around and went to his side, putting her hands on the bed as she bent over him. As she peered at him, she felt a slight movement, and before she could withdraw her hands, they were trapped beneath the Englishman's.

"How dare you take advantage of me so!" she whispered fiercely. "Let go of me."

"Am I in heaven? Are you an angel?" the man quizzed as he gently squeezed her fingers.

"No," responded Roberta roundly. "As you will soon discover if you continue in this fashion."

"Monsieur," Henri said, as he, too, joined Roberta at the bedside. "Are you all right? What has happened? Are you in trouble?"

With seeming reluctance, the Englishman relinquished his hold on Roberta and turned his attention to Henri. "The merest of scratches, my good friend," he replied nonchalantly. "Nothing serious, although I'm afraid my presence here will be discovered by the comte shortly, for I carelessly left a blazing red trail for him to follow."

"He will get no answers from me, monsieur," Henri answered stoutly. "I will send Jacques to hide your horse. You have nothing to fear."

"Except this angel, it would seem. Who are you, mademoiselle?"

"Who—who am I?" Roberta spluttered. "It is the very question I want to ask of you. You—you have the unmitigated impudence to come bursting into my room, disturb my night's rest, take over my bed, and now you want to know who I am? Really, sir, I think you have taken leave of your senses. I demand an immediate explanation of your intrusion; otherwise I shall have to report the entire incident to the proper authorities."

"My angel shows spirit," the man said playfully. "Is she or is she not a vision of true beauty, Henri?"

"Enough!" Roberta said. "I refuse to be drawn into any further discussion of my spirit or beauty. Who are you?"

"Sir Nicholas Thomas, at your service," the Englishman answered promptly. "Pray excuse my tawdry manners in not making the proper leg, but as you can see, I am hand-icapped."

Roberta nodded perfunctorily. The name was unfamiliar, and she saw no reason whatsoever to give it any further acknowledgement. "And how do you propose to explain away your intrusion into my bedroom at such a strange hour?"

"I don't, for I have no wish to embarrass you further, my dear young lady."

Roberta eyed him speculatively, totally unaware of what an alluring picture she made in her shimmering blue night attire. Her hair, still ruffled from sleep, resembled a halo, and her eyes, glinting in the flickering light, sparkled like diamonds.

Suddenly she recalled the conversation she had had ear-lier with Jacques. "The comte's sister!" she exclaimed triumphantly. "Of course! How obtuse I have been."

Henri looked at Sir Nicholas in dismay. "I swear, mon-sieur, I have not said anything."

"I know that, Henri," Sir Nicholas replied curtly. "But as the fair lady seems to know of the compromising position I now find myself in, the need for secrecy appears to be over. Who told you of my affair, mademoiselle?" As he posed the question, there was a steely ring to his voice that caused Roberta to draw back.

"That is none of your business, Sir Nicholas," she re-plied, determined not to be intimidated by his manner. "Although, if you wish to indulge yourself in such cloak-and-dagger activities, I would suggest you be more dis-creet."

"It must have been Jacques, monsieur," Henri interrupted. "Although why he should see fit to prattle on about things that are of no concern to him is beyond my comprehension."

"No matter, Henri," Sir Nicholas said, brushing his brow wearily with his left hand. "The most pressing problem I have at the moment is escaping from the comte and getting back to England. He is bound to have blocked off all routes to Calais, and I'm afraid the wound I have sustained is going to make it impossible for me to travel in any effective disguise. My right arm is useless, and he will have instructed his men to watch for anyone on the move so incapacitated." He lay back in thoughtful silence, watching Roberta from half-closed eyes. "Unless, mademoiselle, you will agree to help me," he added. He spoke so softly that Roberta was certain she had misheard.

"Help you?" she queried in outraged tones, fogetting for a minute that she had suggested this possibility to Mrs. Ashley just a little while earlier. "And why would I want to do that?"

"To save my life. As worthless as most people consider it, I happen to hold it in great esteem."

Roberta looked about her. There was a tenseness to the two men as they waited for her response, and Mrs. Ashley was shaking her head vehemently. Perhaps it was this that decided Roberta, or the encouraging smile that suddenly lit Sir Nicholas's rugged features. Without further consideration, she nodded her head.

"Worthless life or not, Sir Nicholas," she said, "I cannot be party to abetting a Frenchman in dousing it. I suggest we all get a good night's rest and discuss how I may be of assistance on the morrow." Without a backward glance, she joined Mrs. Ashley, who was speechless with horror, and quietly bid the two men good night.

"One moment," Sir Nicholas said, halting her at the doorway. "Does my angel have a name?"

"Miss Rushforth. Roberta Rushforth," she responded. She left with quiet dignity, taking Mrs. Ashley with her.

"Well, I never, Henri," Sir Nicholas exclaimed. "I wonder what her uncle would say if he knew she had agreed to help me."

"*Je ne sais pas, monsieur,*" Henri replied as he quickly

stripped Sir Nicholas of his outer garments. "But I'm certain you will have found a way out of your dilemma by the time you reach England. You have the papers, non? Is that how you received this—this cut?"

Sir Nicholas nodded.

"Perhaps you should tell mademoiselle the truth, then?"

"Never," Sir Nicholas rejoined, "for that would jeopardize the lives of too many people. 'Tis best, methinks, that she believes what Jacques told her. Ignorance is the best defense, should anything go wrong."

chapter 3

BY THE TIME the morning sun was casting its pale-yellow light through the thin muslin curtains of the parlor, Roberta was already enjoying a substantial breakfast. Marie, attending her, didn't hesitate to express her admiration for Roberta's appetite, in view of suffering such a disturbed night.

"That is the very thing that makes me hungry," Roberta responded. "How is the patient? I trust he is recovering?"

Marie shrugged her plump shoulders. "Henri says he is in some pain and unable to move his arm easily. I say he is lucky to be alive. It is not sensible to—to entice a woman like the comte's sister. She is not well liked in these parts," she added as she saw Roberta's inquisitive expression. "And the comte is very possessive of her."

"She must have certain attractions," Roberta said, "else Sir Nicholas wouldn't have taken the risk of incurring the comte's wrath."

"Ah! Indeed, mademoiselle. She is beautiful. But, unfortunately, she is like the rare butterfly, whose name I forget, that feeds only on the leaves of milkweed."

"But I thought milkweed was poisonous to insects," Roberta commented, surprised by the venom in Marie's voice.

"As is her soul," Marie responded firmly. "I have seen what she has done to many of the young men here. But that is not our concern. Sir Nicholas is a determined man and refused to heed my warnings." She retrieved Roberta's empty plate and bustled to the door. "I will bring you some fresh coffee now, *oui?*"

Roberta nodded, sorry that Marie's confidences had ended. She would have liked to have heard more of the beauty Sir Nicholas had risked his life to see. There was something about the story that bothered her. Her first impression of Sir Nicholas had been that he was a forceful person but not foolhardy. And surely only a foolhardy man would have persisted in conducting an illicit liaison with the comte's sister.

Her reverie was rudely interrupted by the sounds of someone banging loudly on the outer door of the inn. The noise echoed down the corridor, bringing her to her feet in haste. It was a noise only a thoughtless person would make so early in the day, a person who cared not at all for anyone else's desire to sleep. She was about to open the parlor door and find out the cause of the commotion, when Marie appeared.

"Oh! Mademoiselle, please stay here," she whispered in great agitation. "It's the comte. Henri will see what he wants."

"Indeed? I think I want to see this comte for myself," Roberta responded with spirit. "Anyone who displays such bad manners deserves to be rebuked."

"Non—non—Please don't go," Marie said as she tried unsuccessfully to block the doorway. "Sir Nicholas would not like it, I'm sure."

"Nonsense, Marie. You stay here if you wish, but I'm not going to. This is the first piece of excitement that has come my way in the longest time, and I refuse to turn my back on it."

She swept past Marie and reached the corridor just as Henri withdrew the last bolt from the front door. She stood back in the shadows as he swung the heavy oak door open, and she was able to get a clear look at the comte.

He was very tall and distinguished. His thick black hair, swept backward in a style similar to Sir Nicholas's, was caught at his nape by a black ribbon. His brows, black and menacing, were pulled together in a frown, and in his left hand a riding crop was raised as if he were readying himself to pound the door again. His dress was all black except for the white relief of his stock, which fell in careful folds over his riding jacket. Even the three rings on his fingers were black. Roberta shuddered. He was not a man she would care to cross.

He glowered down at Henri and appeared to consider him for the longest time, in much the same way a bird would consider a worm. Henri stood his ground, and Roberta was impressed by this show of defiance.

"Bonjour, Monsieur le Comte," Henri said pleasantly. "Do we have the pleasure of serving you breakfast this morning?"

"Mon dieu!" the comte said, his teeth clenched. "You know why I'm here. Do not make the mistake of thinking me a fool. I know you are harboring the Englishman. The one my men injured last night as he fled my sister's boudoir. Take me to him immediately."

Henri shrugged his shoulders, and Roberta imagined the bewildered look he must be presenting. "I'm afraid I don't understand you, Monsieur le Comte. We have no one of that description staying here. You must be mistaken."

The comte brought his riding crop down savagely on the doorpost. "I will not bear with your lies, you idiot. Stand back and let me search this place myself." He pushed past Henri and strode toward the stairs.

Roberta glimpsed the dismay on Henri's face as he swung around and tried to stop the comte. She quickly emerged from her hiding place.

"Ah! There you are, Henri," she said, ignoring the comte, who had his foot on the first stair. "My father would like you to help ready him for our journey. But"—she turned slowly and acknowledged the comte's presence by inclining her head graciously in his direction—"if you are busy, I shall tell him to have patience."

She moved toward the comte, forcing him to retreat. He bowed low, and she dimpled her cheeks in an engaging smile.

"Thank you," she said. "You know how it is with old people. They do so hate to be kept waiting."

"Of course, mademoiselle," the comte replied, his voice softening perceptibly. "I hope I didn't disturb his rest just now, with my loud knocking. I didn't know Henri had any other guests last night apart from my *friend*."

Roberta raised her finely arched brow at this remark and

then laughed, a low, melodious sound that filled the hallway.

"'Pon rep!" she exclaimed. "And I thought we had the inn to ourselves. Had I known that we shared it with such a boisterous party, I would have found something quieter." Her smile took the sting from her words. "Excuse me," she continued. "Please do not let me keep you." She made a small curtsy and walked slowly up the stairs.

The comte stared at her retreating back as she entered Sir Nicholas's room.

"Papa," he heard her say, "a very nice man is most apologetic lest his noisy arrival disturbed you. Henri will be here directly, and then we can be on our way." The door closed.

"You have no objections, I trust, Henri, if I look into the other rooms?"

Henri shook his head. "No, it is as I said, Monsieur le Comte. It is just the young lady, her father, and a woman companion staying here. I beg that you don't burst into the old lady's room. She will not take kindly to such an intrusion; of that I can assure you."

The comte hesitated and looked up the stairs. The barely audible voices of two people engaged in conversation filtered down. He turned and faced Henri squarely.

"If you have lied to me, my friend," he snarled, "and it comes to my attention that you have been harboring this fugitive, you will pay dearly."

A pained expression flitted across Henri's face. "Would I dare to misinform you, Monsieur le Comte? But please, don't take my word. Have a look around the inn."

"No, you fool, I don't want to bear with the ravings of an aging English lady. Just remember, you will suffer if I find out you have lied to me."

He stormed out, slamming the door behind him, and Henri stood where he was until Marie joined him.

"Mon dieu, Henri," she cried. "What will become of us if he should ever discover the truth?" She clung to him for support. "I told you I wanted no part of Sir Nicholas's liaison with that woman. No one interferes with the comte's family without suffering."

"Now, Marie," Henri admonished gently, "this is not the

time to draw back. Sir Nicholas is a good man, and we have promised to help him. Take heart from Mlle. Rushforth's attitude. What a magnificent drama she played! You should have seen how quickly she tamed the comte. Come, let us congratulate her."

When they reached Sir Nicholas's room, they found the door locked. Before Henri could knock, they heard Roberta's voice, raised in scolding tones.

"She must think we are the comte," Henri whispered admiringly. "Hear the exasperation in her voice. I begin to feel confident that Sir Nicholas will manage his escape to England after all."

Henri knocked on the door and identified himself. The key was turned, and Roberta peered out cautiously.

"Has that dreadful man gone?" she whispered.

Marie nodded. "Henri told him that your companion was likely to throw a hysterical fit if he disturbed her, so he decided against searching our inn. Oh! Mademoiselle Rushforth, how can we ever thank you enough for what you did?" She stretched up and kissed Roberta on the cheek.

Roberta hugged the little Frenchwoman and laughed in delight. "I haven't enjoyed myself so much in an age," she said. She stepped back and opened the door wide. "Come in," she said.

Sir Nicholas was still in bed. Three pillows were propping him up in a sitting position, and in his right hand was a small pistol.

"You can put that murderous thing down," Roberta said as Henri and Marie entered. "Your inquisitive friend has gone."

"But you are wrong to assume that you have nothing more to fear," Henri cautioned. "The comte is a dangerous man and is used to having his own way. I'm afraid for you, mademoiselle. He took you in great liking."

But Roberta was not to be frightened. "There is nothing he can do to me," she declared. "Why, if he tried to waylay me, it would cause a diplomatic furor. My uncle would see to that."

"I think Henri has overstated the case," Sir Nicholas replied calmly, frowning at the innkeeper. "However, I think it in our best interests to depart immediately, although, if we are to give any credence to your story, Miss Rushforth, we can hardly dash along pell-mell to Calais. I will instruct your coachman to drive at a sedate pace, so that if any of the comte's men are watching the turnpikes, we will not arouse their suspicions."

"*I* will tell Williams," Roberta retorted, annoyed by his presumptuous attitude. "He does not take kindly to receiving orders from strangers. In fact, if you have no objections, Sir Nicholas, I will have to tell him who you really are, else he might refuse to take you up in our carriage. He's an old man, and a mite set in his ways."

"He's as stubborn as they come," Henri concurred, "but he'll not give any secrets away. You can trust him, Sir Nicholas."

Sir Nicholas shrugged. "'Twould seem I have no choice," he said with seeming nonchalance. "Appeal to his patriotic senses, I beg you, Miss Rushforth, if he shows any signs of refusing."

"He won't," Roberta replied with more conviction than she felt. "I will arrange things to everyone's satisfaction. Perhaps, Henri, you could help *age* Sir Nicholas." She stood back and critically surveyed the gentleman. "I think by at least twenty years, don't you? He must look old enough to be my father, in case we are stopped. And, Marie, would you be kind enough to prepare us a hamper of food? I fear it would be unwise for us to stop more often than we must."

Sir Nicholas smiled his appreciation at these arrangements and watched Roberta with approval as she left the room.

"I do believe I'm going to enjoy the next few days," he murmured as Henri helped him out of bed. "She's a remarkable lady, isn't she, Henri?"

He might not have been so cheerful had he been privy to Roberta's conversation with Mrs. Ashley. That good lady, having spent a sleepless night, was in no mood to listen to Roberta's request that she ready herself for an immediate departure.

"I'm not feeling very well, Roberta," she complained. She did, indeed, look pale. "I had no sleep at all, for just as I was dozing off, a great hullabaloo started, with some mad Frenchman banging on the door as if he were intent on bringing it down. That, on top of the events of last night, is too much for my delicate constitution to tolerate."

"I know, Ashley, but I'm afraid we have no alternative. We have to leave for Calais this morning. It is too dangerous for Sir Nicholas to spend another hour here. That madman you referred to was the comte." She refrained from mentioning her part in the earlier drama.

"Really, Roberta," Mrs Ashley protested faintly. "You mustn't get yourself embroiled in this. Lord Bromley will be very, very angry."

"He would be angry if he heard that we refused to help an Englishman," she responded. "Come along, Ashley," she urged. "It will only be for a few days, just until we are safely aboard the packet to Dover. Sir Nicholas won't need our help once he is on English soil."

"You can hardly abandon him then," Mrs. Ashley argued illogically. "He's injured. He may still need our assistance."

"Then you agree?" Roberta asked, and when Mrs. Ashley nodded, she hugged her. "Thank you. I don't care what Sir Nicholas's reason is for escaping; I'm just glad we can be of use, for I found the comte to be a bully."

Mrs. Ashley fixed a penetrating stare on Roberta. "When did you meet him?" she asked shrewdly.

"Only in a manner of speaking," Roberta answered quickly. "I overheard him shouting at Henri. He sounded highly intolerant."

"And what did he look like?" There was a lively curiosity to Mrs. Ashley's voice that surprised Roberta.

"Satanic!" she replied, and then inclined her head thoughtfully. "Why do you ask?"

"I have the strangest feeling that we haven't seen the last of him. No matter. And has Williams agreed to another passenger?"

"Yes. I had to use a little more persuasion than with you, Ashley. He is willing enough now, though."

She recalled the conversation she had had with her coachman a little while back. It had been an odd one. Williams had only relented when she had mentioned Sir Nicholas by name. Indeed, now that she thought about it, she was certain Williams had recognized the name.

She would ask her uncle about it when she arrived in England. If anyone knew anything, he would, and she couldn't deny that she was developing an interest in Sir Nicholas.

chapter 4

ROBERTA WATCHED WILLIAMS from the open doorway of the inn as he checked to see if the horses were properly harnessed. It was always a pleasure to witness his strong, capable hands working in such an expert way.

"Does everything pass muster, Williams?" she called out.

He straightened up and nodded. "I'm about finished here," he replied. "I'll just go upstairs and see if I can be of any use there. Sommat tells me Henri could use a bit of help."

Roberta laughed. "Papa is not that infirm," she said, finding it difficult to believe that Sir Nicholas would accept the helping hands of two men well into their fifties. He would look far too undignified, and that, she felt, wouldn't suit his arrogant soul one whit. "But you had best go and check Henri's handiwork," she added softly as Williams passed her. "I left him in charge of aging Sir Nicholas. Don't forget, he is supposed to be my father."

"Very good, Miss Roberta. I'll do as you suggest."

Roberta retreated to the parlor to wait. She had long since finished readying herself for the journey, and all she had left to do was put on her bonnet. It was perched on the back of one of the settles, and she eyed it now in delight. It was a gay little thing, all netting, feathers and flowers. She had almost decided against buying it, because it had been expensive, but she was glad now that she had. It suited her present adventurous mood to perfection. She ran her finger down one of the feathers just as Mrs. Ashley joined her.

"Surely you're not going to wear that, Roberta," Mrs. Ashley exclaimed. "It would be such a shame if you ruined it before we got to England."

"I can't imagine why you think I'll spoil it, Ashley. After all, I shall be sitting in the carriage all day. Anyway, it suits my present mood."

"But you'll only draw attention to yourself," Mrs. Ashley said, shaking her head. "And that, I should think, would have been the last thing you wished to do, on account of our extra passenger."

"Nonsense, Ashley. That's the very thing I'm striving for. If we are stopped by the comte or any of his men, I don't want them to look at anyone but me. Now, don't worry," she added hastily as a worried look settled on Mrs. Ashley's face. "We probably won't encounter anybody, but it is better to be prepared." She broke off as she heard a noise outside and turned toward the door. "Ah! That must be Sir Nicholas."

She placed her bonnet on a side table, then walked into the corridor and watched with amusement as Sir Nicholas made his way slowly down the stairs. He was flanked by Williams and Henri and, in a voice she didn't recognize, was testily issuing orders to Williams for fresh hot bricks to be placed in the carriage.

"You can never trust these damned Frenchies to do the right thing, Williams," he said with a fine disregard for Henri's feelings. "They have no idea about creature comforts, except when it comes to filling their bellies with wine."

The change in Sir Nicholas was miraculous, and Roberta marveled at the transformation. His shoulders, seemingly bowed with age, forced him into a low stoop. A clever stance, she thought approvingly, for it made him appear to be a good six inches shorter than his natural height. He leaned heavily on a silver cane, which he grasped with his left hand. His right arm rested on his lower back. There was no trace of his copper hair. It was now white, as were his brows. Deep lines were carved in his cheeks, and more hugged the corners of his eyes and mouth. His clothes she recognized immediately as those belonging to Williams. He looked very much as though he were an eccentric old man who gave no thought to his appearance.

When he finally reached the bottom stair, Roberta clapped in delight. Sir Nicholas stood up and made an elegant leg. His eyes, the only feature she recognized, were brimming with laughter. Then the sound of someone entering the inn caused him to bend over again, and in a querulous voice he ordered her to his side. She complied quickly and placed herself protectively at his right elbow.

"You've kept me waiting long enough, Roberta," he said for the benefit of the visitor. "And where is that woman Ashley? I hope she is not still complaining about the noise that awoke us all this morning."

"Papa, please don't work yourself up so. Ashley has been ready for the longest time. See, here she is now. Come, Ashley," Roberta continued quickly as she caught sight of the stranger, who now stood in the corridor, effectively blocking their exit. "Papa is anxious to make Bethune by nightfall."

She led the way down the passageway, relinquishing her position at Sir Nicholas's side to Williams. Mrs. Ashley brought up the rear with Henri. As Roberta drew level with the man, she stared at him haughtily, and when he made no attempt to move, she waved her hand in an imperious gesture.

"If you will excuse us, sir," she said, and breathed a sigh of relief when at last he stood back. She passed him without so much as a nod, and when she judged that Williams and Sir Nicholas would be level with him, turned back. "My bonnet!" she cried. "I forgot my bonnet!"

As she pushed her way back to the parlor, she was pleased to note that the stranger gave Sir Nicholas and Williams no more than a cursory look. His eyes were on her. She quickly donned her bonnet, and was still tying the strings as she emerged from the parlor. The man was standing where she had left him, but this time as she passed, he moved back of his own accord and bowed.

"C'est magnifique, mademoiselle," he murmured as she sailed by him for the second time.

There was a further delay as Sir Nicholas sent Henri back three times to reheat the bricks. In a low voice that only Roberta, who was now seated next to him, could hear, Sir

Nicholas explained that he had recognized the stranger as being one of the comte's servants.

"I don't think it in our best interest to appear in any great haste to leave."

"At this rate, we will be lucky if we set out before noon," Roberta quipped. "Take pity on Henri and accept the bricks he offers next time."

"As you wish, although I happen to think all that un-accustomed exercise is good for him." He paused to clear his throat. "I haven't thanked you yet for coming to my rescue just now. Your timing was perfect."

"Think nothing of it, Sir Nicholas," she responded, a faint blush coloring her cheeks at his admiring tone. "I find I'm enjoying myself enormously. For the past six months, I have been forced to endure my own company, and I must confess, it has become prodigiously dreary."

Sir Nicholas looked at her in surprise and seemed about to ask why, when Mrs. Ashley claimed Roberta's attention by moaning pitifully. Roberta quickly moved over and sat next to her companion. "What is it, Ashley?" she asked. "Are you all right?"

"I'll be all right once we are on our way, Roberta. It was that man, who made me feel all faint. The way he looked at you sent a shiver right down my spine."

"Demmed insolent cur," Sir Nicholas growled. "That's another fault with the French. They have no manners worth speaking of." He stuck his head out of the open window and shouted for Henri, who was already scurrying across the courtyard with the offending bricks clasped tightly to his chest.

Williams opened the door, and Henri's face appeared. He looked up anxiously as he deftly placed the bricks around Sir Nicholas's feet. "I am positive the comte sent his man here to check the validity of Mlle. Rushforth's story," he said softly. "He doesn't suspect a thing. However, I think you had best not return for a while, Sir Nicholas. It would not be safe. The comte will have someone watching my inn for several weeks; of that you can be certain."

Roberta, straining to hear the conversation, caught only the last part and was intrigued. Sir Nicholas, however, merely growled and dismissed Henri brusquely.

Henri's face disappeared, the door was slammed shut, and they were on their way. Sir Nicholas shut his eyes and held his injured arm. Roberta could sense it hurt him and suggested he put his feet up on the seat and stretch out.

"I think not, Miss Rushforth," he answered. "If we are stopped, it might arouse suspicion. However, if you could contrive to push an extra cushion under this wretched arm of mine, that might ease the pain."

Henri had thoughtfully supplied plenty of pillows, and Roberta wedged a few of them about his injured limb. "I think that will absorb most of the jolts and bumps," she said. "Does it throb dreadfully?"

"Quite," he replied, opening his eyes. "But if you sit across from me, the sight of that absurd confection atop your head will take my mind off it entirely."

Roberta laughed but did as he requested, while Mrs. Ashley clucked disapprovingly.

They journeyed on in silence. Sir Nicholas dozed fitfully, and Mrs. Ashley busied herself with her tatting. Roberta tried to read, but couldn't concentrate. Her mind, as if with a will of its own, kept wandering over the events of last night. Nothing made sense. She was still engaged in trying to pull Sir Nicholas's story apart, when the carriage halted abruptly.

Mrs. Ashley immediately dropped her half-finished doily on the floor and looked fearfully toward the window. Sir Nicholas opened his eyes and quickly hunched himself over, half turning his back to the window. Roberta picked up her book and made a great pretense of being deeply involved in its pages.

A few moments later, a man dressed in military uniform rode up. He opened the door of the carriage, and the three occupants stared at him with varying degrees of outrage.

"How dare you intrude on our privacy, young man! Close the door immediately," Sir Nicholas roared. "I don't know when I have been so rudely treated."

"There, there, Papa," Roberta said, "I'm sure there must be a good reason for this stoppage." She turned back toward the soldier and leaned forward slightly, enough to shield Sir Nicholas from any penetrating stare. "Can we help you, sir?" she inquired, and then repeated it in French when he looked confused, adding, "Have you lost something, perhaps?"

The soldier, obviously enchanted by the picture she presented, smiled at her nervously. "I am so sorry to have intruded, mademoiselle. In truth, we are searching for a fugitive—a man some five and thirty years, with an injured right arm."

Roberta shook her head, her eyes wide with apparent fear. "Is he dangerous?" she asked, her voice breathless.

"Desperate, ruthless even, so I have been told," the young soldier answered. "But I doubt he will bother *you*. I'm sure he couldn't have reached this far, but we have orders to stop everyone."

"Roberta," Sir Nicholas interrupted impatiently, "whatever it is that you find of such great interest, I demand you cease your inquiries. I will not tolerate such ragged manners from anyone, and to be disturbed in the middle of my rest by some whippersnapper who can do no more than ogle you in the most disgusting fashion is outside of enough!"

Roberta smiled her apologies at the young man. As he hadn't understood a word, for Sir Nicholas had spoken in English, he returned her smile warmly. "You have seen no one of that description?" he asked.

Roberta shook her head. "As you can see, we only have two men in our party. Williams, the coachman, and Papa, who suffers terribly from gout."

"Whither are you bound, mademoiselle?" he asked.

"Calais. We are returning to England after spending the past six months in Switzerland." She put her hand to her chest and coughed slightly. "I have been there for treatment."

A command from behind the soldier caused him to stiffen, and with obvious reluctance, he started to shut the door. "I hope you are fully recovered, mademoiselle," he said, then slammed the door and galloped away.

"Really, Roberta," Mrs. Ashley said, "I'm appalled by your behavior. I would never have believed you were capable of conducting yourself so wantonly." Her anger had seemingly chased away her previous fears.

"But Ashley," Roberta protested, trying hard not to laugh, "I was only trying to keep the young man's attention from Sir Nicholas. I would never dream of behaving so flirtatiously in London."

Mrs. Ashley subsided into her corner and sighed. "I just hope Lord Bromley will understand and forgive me for being so gullible. I can't imagine why I let you get embroiled in this farrago. There's no saying where it will end."

"In England, Mrs. Ashley," Sir Nicholas replied humorously, in an attempt to ease her distress. "That is, if my gout doesn't flare up again."

"I can see I am wasting my time," Mrs. Ashley snapped. "It is apparent that neither of you, Sir Nicholas, nor you, Roberta, are in the mood to acknowledge that every minute we spend on French soil is a dangerous one." She sniffed loudly and resumed her tatting. The only indication of her extreme displeasure was the speed with which her fingers plied the shuttle.

Roberta and Sir Nicholas exchanged bemused glances.

"Tell me, Sir Nicholas," Roberta said after a suitable pause, "what are you really escaping from?"

"The comte's anger," he replied, suppressing a yawn with difficulty. "He is known to have an ungovernable temper."

"I find that hard to accept. I don't believe an affair of the heart would cause such a pother." She eyed him skeptically. "There must be something more than you're telling."

"And what do you know of such affairs?" Sir Nicholas quizzed in a jocular fashion. "Nothing, I'm sure. A genteel lady would have been sheltered from such knowledge." He spoke softly, and his voice only just carried to Roberta over the noise of the wheels.

"Good heavens, Sir Nicholas!" Roberta exclaimed impatiently. "I'm not a maiden just out of the schoolroom. I have seen more Seasons than I care to admit, and am fully cognizant of the affairs that most of my married friends indulge in."

"Then you must also be aware that when one's family honor has been besmirched, a man will go to great lengths to avenge it. Such is the case with the comte."

"Now I really do not comprehend why you are running away. I always understood such matters were settled by a duel."

"But the scandal, Miss Rushforth!" Sir Nicholas said in horrified tones. "If I killed the comte, as I surely would be forced to, I doubt I would ever get out of France. He is a man with enormous power in his country, even if he is not well liked. No, Miss Rushforth, 'tis the idea of being forced to languish in a French jail that is causing me to flee now."

Roberta leaned back and sighed. It seemed pointless, trying to prise the truth out of him. If he wanted to be thought a coward, that was his affair. She stole a glance at his profile and was annoyed to see that he was smiling at her.

"Really, Sir Nicholas, you are displaying an offending lack of concern over your present predicament. I would have expected you to be abject in your demeanor and to show Mrs. Ashley and myself more gratitude for helping effect your cowardly escape."

Sir Nicholas's smile broadened into a grin, which infuriated Roberta further.

"Handicapped as I am, Miss Rushforth, I cannot show you how truly grateful I am. But, please, I beg you to accept my thanks. It is sincere, I do assure you."

Roberta refused to be mollified, and to show how out of patience she was with him, she turned away slightly. She felt certain that he was enjoying a huge joke at her expense, and she didn't like it at all. Even Stephen had never dared goad her when her temper was roused. Dear, dear Stephen had known how to treat her. She felt the familiar constriction of her heart as she thought of him, and suddenly wondered what she was going to do when she met him again. A meeting would be inevitable when she resumed her place in Society, for they still shared many friends. She sighed again.

Mrs. Ashley could tell at a glance that the bleakness of Roberta's face was caused by thoughts of Stephen Davenport, but Sir Nicholas, who was not privy to the secrets of Roberta's heart, could only speculate about her sudden change of mood. He swiftly concluded that she was regretting her hasty decision to aid him—one, he was certain, she had only taken to annoy Mrs. Ashley. If that were the case, then he would have to take care not to rile her further. It was imperative that he reach England as quickly as possible, and she offered him the only hope of achieving his goal.

"Forgive me, Miss Rushforth," he said contritely. "I don't mean to seem evasive. You must put my reluctance to talk plainly of such matters down to my natural reticence in embroiling ladies of your station in my personal affairs. I find it difficult to discuss them and am afraid of causing you further offense."

Roberta inclined her head slightly, indicating that she accepted his apology. In truth, she was beginning to feel ashamed of her outburst. "My curiosity is to blame," she replied, recalling how Stephen used to tease her about it and warn her that she would be termed a meddlesome busybody if she didn't curb her inquiring mind. "Your business is no concern of mine, although, in my own defense, I would hazard a guess that you grew up without sisters." She paused long enough for Sir Nicholas to acknowledge the truth of her statement and ask how she knew. "It is quite apparent that you have no real understanding of the fairer sex. Had you had even one sister, you would realize that all young girls delight in gossiping about the way their brothers kick up their heels and squander money in riotous living. They know a lot more than you would ever dream about the charms of the ballet girls, paramours and such, even if they choose to profess innocence."

"Indeed, Miss Rushforth!" he exclaimed, genuinely intrigued. "I would never have believed it. I don't think I've ever directed a thought to what young ladies talk about. I suppose, unconsciously, I have always assumed that they were too involved in absorbing the intricacies of running a household in preparation for their marriages, to have the time to consider what their brothers were up to."

"An antiquated notion, Sir Nicholas," Roberta responded. "Modern ladies are far better educated than their predecessors, and well read in Greek and Latin. And it is the classics, Sir Nicholas, that feed their imagination. There is little they don't know of Roman orgies and Greek perversions, and they assume, rightly or wrongly, that if men indulged in such passions centuries ago, they still do today. Personally, I don't believe all men are such hedonists. My uncle, for instance, and many of his friends and acquaintances, are serious-minded and concern themselves with the extreme poverty suffered by a large portion of the population in England. But"—she shrugged her shoulders—"that is a topic that most people shy away from, and certainly not one that is discussed in many drawing rooms today."

"I'm afraid my ignorance on that matter leaves me little else to say," Sir Nicholas murmured, and closed his eyes as though he were too weary to continue the conversation. The truth was that he knew a lot more than Roberta. However, he'd best be prudent, and so maintained his silence. If he allowed himself to inform her just what was being done to ease the plight of the poor, and his involvement in these plans, it would lend a lie to the image of his being a roué that he had striven so hard to give.

Roberta looked at him with disdain for a moment, and then resumed her study of the countryside. She should have known better than to try to conduct a serious conversation with a man of such rakish persuasions, she thought ruefully, and then followed his example and closed her eyes.

She was soon fast asleep, and only woke when Williams stopped and announced that they had arrived at Bethune, where they were to spend the night.

chapter 5

By the time the party was ensconced in the carriage the next morning, it was evident that Roberta's ill humor concerning Sir Nicholas had evaporated. It appeared that her only concern was whether the comte was following them.

"You appear to have a certain knowledge of his character, Sir Nicholas. Is it likely that he would give up his search for you so easily?" she inquired.

"He has probably decided that he has a better chance of finding me if he watches every boat that leaves Calais, instead of searching every carriage that passes through Le Cateau bound for Calais."

"So we might not have seen the last of him, then?" she pressed.

"Anything is possible, Miss Rushforth, but once we are aboard the packet, we can safely assume that he won't bother us again."

"Then I pray we accomplish that without mishap," Mrs. Ashley said fervently, "for I have no desire to meet this man."

Her prayers were answered late in the afternoon, for they boarded the boat without delay. Williams managed to persuade the captain to assign his party three of the best staterooms, and settled them in before he went off to superintend the unloading of the carriage.

From her porthole, Roberta viewed the bustle on the quayside with interest. Young boys, staggering under the weight of large trunks, scurried up the gangplank, while the owners of the luggage stood about in small groups, waiting until the last possible moment to board. No one, it seemed to Roberta, was in a hurry to leave France. No one, that is, except Sir Nicholas.

Strong male voices, shouting directions, penetrated the thin walls of her cabin, and finally she heard the noise of the heavy chain anchor being weighed. The gangplank was drawn in, and all activity on the quayside seemed to stop. They were off at last, and she sighed in relief.

Suddenly a loud shout broke the silence, and Roberta saw a man hidden under a black-and-gold cape of hideous design trying to attract the captain's attention. Seconds later, the gangplank was lowered, and the man boarded. The packet then left the safety of the harbor and was soon plying its way over the choppy waters of the English Channel.

Darkness had fallen by the time boredom drove Roberta from her cabin. Mrs. Ashley was prostrate on her bunk with seasickness, moaning her misery for anyone who cared to hear. There was nothing Roberta could do to help the poor woman, so she wandered up onto the top deck and held the rail for support. A full moon cast its luminous light over the boat. The North Star was bright, and she stared upward, trying to identify the constellations.

"It is an awesome sight, mademoiselle, *n'est ce pas?*"

The familiar voice of the comte caused a shock wave to ripple through her body, and she gripped the rail tightly. What a fool she had been to leave the safety of her cabin. And how stupid to think they had escaped him!

"It is Mlle. Rushforth, isn't it?" he continued smoothly, oblivious to the look of horror on her face. "I met you yesterday in Le Cateau."

Roberta nodded in a dreamlike fashion and wondered how he had discovered her name. She wanted to pinch herself to make certain she was awake and not suffering some terrible nightmare. But the awful reality of her situation was borne swiftly home when she felt him grip her elbow. His fingers were like a steel trap, and she suddenly felt as vulnerable as any caught animal.

"Would you care for a stroll, perhaps?" he asked. "You might take a chill if you just stand in this cold wind. After your recent illness, I think that would not be advised."

"No—no, thank you, Monsieur le Comte. I—I have been away from my cabin too long as it is. Ashley and Papa will be worried." She tried to pull her arm free, but his grasp was relentless.

"Ah, yes! Your papa. How is he? I trust he has weathered the journey well."

Roberta shivered involuntarily at his menacing tone. "Amazingly well," she replied with as much indifference as she could muster. "Though he did work himself up into a rage when we were stopped by some soldiers." She broke off and gave a shrill laugh. "But, how silly of me. You must have heard about that, and about my ailment, from the young man who questioned us. Do you happen to now if they found the person they were seeking?"

The comte appeared to weigh the seeming innocence of her question. Then, evidently deciding that it was genuine, he laughed. "You are extremely quick-witted, mademoiselle," he said admiringly. "I did, indeed, hear of your recent sojourn in Switzerland from the young man. But, to answer your question, no, the person we are looking for has not yet been apprehended."

"He must have committed a terrible crime, for the army to be involved in the search. In England, the army would only be called into service for such a search if the fugitive had committed a crime of high treason."

"Ah! I see your meaning. It is the same in France. The man we are looking for is a traitor. A spy!"

"No!" Roberta exclaimed, and struggled to hide the amusement she felt at such an outrageous claim. "Really! How simply terrifying. I hope you catch up with him. I can't bear to think that such men get away."

"He won't," the comte assured her. "Our net is widespread, and he won't slip through it."

The confidence with which he spoke caused a feeling of apprehension to well up inside her. Suddenly she realized he had spoken the truth about his reasons for hunting Sir Nicholas. She inhaled deeply to steady her nerves and tried to grasp the import of what she had just learned. But her mind refused to function. She felt only an overwhelming desire to rid herself of the comte's presence and to warn Sir Nicholas.

"I hope my careless revelations have not alarmed you, Mademoiselle Rushforth," the comte said in the face of her continuing silence. "I will personally insure that you are not harmed."

"You—you mean he is on this boat?" Roberta asked, acting the part of a frightened lady without difficulty. She *was* frightened, not for herself, but for Sir Nicholas.

"So I have been informed. That is why I am confident we will succeed in capturing him. If it is true that he is here, he is trapped." He laughed again, revealing several black teeth and finally relinquishing his grasp on her arm. "Allow me to escort you back to your cabin, Mademoiselle Rushforth. I would never forgive myself if anything happened to you."

"Thank you," Roberta murmured faintly. "You're very kind, but I don't think it necessary. I don't think Ashley would approve if she knew I had been talking to a stranger."

"Hardly a stranger," he replied in a caressing voice. "After all, we have met before."

"But—but we were not introduced," Roberta responded quickly. She could feel the small hairs at her nape rising as he stepped closer and placed his hands intimately on her shoulders.

"Perhaps this will seal our meeting," he whispered, and brought his mouth down to meet hers. She twisted her head sharply, but his lips, wet and pressing, touched her cheek.

"Please, Monsieur le Comte," she managed with more composure than she dreamed possible, "don't be so silly. I'll excuse your action this time, because of the moon's fullness, but I hope, if we should ever meet again, you will act more like a gentleman."

She turned and fled, only stopping for breath when she had reached Sir Nicholas's cabin. Giving no more than a perfunctory knock, she entered. Such was her state of agitation that she gave no thought to the impropriety of entering a gentleman's room. He was seated at a small table bolted to the floor by the porthole, peering intently at some papers. He looked up at that moment and hurriedly pulled the papers together, failing to notice one sheet flutter to the floor. She watched it float slowly down and in that moment decided against repeating the comte's allegations. She would consult with her uncle, Lord Bromley, first, for how could she be certain what Sir Nicholas was really up to? His behavior was odd, to say the least, and if the comte was to be believed, he was not a man to be trusted.

"Good evening, Miss Rushforth," Sir Nicholas said, smiling at her lazily. "Do you make a habit of entering a man's room unchaperoned?"

She waited for the pounding of her heart to subside before nodding. "It's a habit I picked up from you, Papa," she responded lightly. "I have come to inform you that the comte is on board. I have just left him on the top deck."

"Indeed," was the noncommittal reply. "Does Mrs. Ashley know you went for a walk alone?"

"I'm no longer a young girl who needs to ask persmission to go for a walk," she said with considerable irritation. "Had I known how you would react, I wouldn't have bothered to come and warn you."

"As it happens, Miss Rushforth, I'm aware of his presence. I saw him come on board. He was the late arrival."

The maddeningly calm way in which he spoke caused Roberta to mutter angrily that he couldn't possibly have recognized the comte under the heavy cloak he had worn.

"Oh! But it was the cloak that I identified. The comte is the only person I know who would sport something so vulgar."

"Yet you don't seem in the least bit agitated," Roberta ventured, trying hard to match his casual attitude. "I would have thought that, knowing of his presence, you would have taken the precaution of locking your door."

"There, I grant you, I made a mistake. However, as no harm has come because of my thoughtlessness, there is little to worry about." He stood up and clumsily collected the papers, which he then thrust inside his jacket. "I think I will retire now, Miss Rushforth, and try to get some sleep before we land."

"Of course, Sir Nicholas," Roberta replied, eyeing the single sheet of paper still on the floor. It lay no more than a few feet from her. "Perhaps you should check your porthole first, though, and make certain it is secure." He nodded his agreement, and as soon as he turned his back, she retrieved the paper and quickly hid it in the folds of her dress. "Good night," she said, and before he had a chance to respond, she departed.

Once in the privacy of her own cabin, she pulled the paper out and smoothed it with trembling fingers. She studied it carefully, but it made no sense to her. It appeared to be a list, written in fine copperplate, but the letters were a jumble and formed no recognizable words.

"It must be in code," she breathed, her eyes glinting with excitement. "Oh, Sir Nicholas, what a careless man you are!"

She sat down at a table similar to the one in Sir Nicholas's cabin and searched the drawer for writing implements. Dipping the pen into the ink, she slowly copied the letters onto a fresh sheet of paper, stopping frequently to check that she had made no mistake. When she finished and was satisfied that all was in order, she carefully folded her copy and tucked it into the top of her chemise, where it lay like a cold, sharp knife against her bosom. She returned the original to her dress pocket.

"Now all I have to do is wait for a suitable opportunity to return it to you, Sir Nicholas," she murmured, "and I hope one arises before you discover it is missing."

She lay on her bunk, fully dressed, and stared at the ceiling, far too excited to sleep. She had a lot to think about. She had to find a plausible reason to persuade Sir Nicholas to accompany them to London, for she now felt it imperative that she not lose sight of him until she had spoken to her uncle. Lord Bromley, in his capacity as Under Secretary, would know exactly how to handle such an unusual situation.

She jerked up into a sitting position some five minutes later, a self-satisfied expression on her face. "The comte, of course! He would be most suspicious if he noticed that I had left my father at Dover," she exclaimed triumphantly. "Sir Nicholas, you'll just *have* to accept my offer to take you to London."

chapter 6

IT WAS EARLY afternoon before the boat finally reached Dover. The trip had been rough, and as far as Roberta could determine from the faces of the people who had gathered on deck, she was one of the few lucky ones who had not suffered seasickness. There was no sign of Mrs. Ashley or Sir Nicholas, and she assumed they were still in their cabins. As she stood, looking toward land, Williams came up behind her.

"That was as rough a trip as I've ever 'ad," he said. "I expect Mrs. Ashley is glad it's over."

Roberta turned guiltily. She really hadn't given a thought to Mrs. Ashley's discomfort, for she had devoted all her energy to the problems Sir Nicholas presented. "I expect so, Williams," she replied. "She never has liked sea voyages. I take it you didn't suffer unduly?"

"Nay, not me, Miss Roberta. Matter of fact, I rather enjoyed the battle we had with the elements. I looked in on . . . oh . . . your papa just a short while ago, and he's all ready for the journey to London."

"You mean he wants to join us?" she exclaimed. "I—I thought he would have preferred to make his own arrangements, and travel alone."

Williams looked about cautiously before mumbling, "It was his suggestion, Miss Roberta. He thought it for the best on account of the comte being on board. It would look very strange if you were seen going off without your father, he said."

Roberta nodded in satisfaction, pleased that this hurdle had been jumped without trouble.

"Sir Nicholas even asked if it would be possible to make Reigate by dusk," Williams added, "for he knows of a very good inn there where we could spend the night."

"And can we?" she inquired, fingering the piece of paper in her pocket. She wondered if Sir Nicholas had noticed it was missing yet.

"With the fresh team that should be awaiting us, I'm sure of it. I'll just give them their heads."

"Good. Now, as for getting ashore, we will wait for you in Papa's cabin, and when you have the carriage ready, you can fetch us. The captain won't mind our lingering if you make it worth his while, will he?"

"I've already taken care of that, Miss Roberta. Your father gave the necessary funds." He tipped his tricorn and left Roberta in deep thought.

"It would seem that Sir Nicholas and I think along the same lines," she said. "Now I am forced to wonder why he wants to go to Reigate."

The answer to that was obvious when they arrived at the inn. The landlord, after Sir Nicholas had spoken quietly in his ear, greeted the party warmly.

"An old and trustworthy friend," Sir Nicholas said when Roberta asked what it was all about. "He'll take very good care of us, and I can promise you an excellent meal. People come from miles around to enjoy the hospitality he offers."

"A safe haven, indeed," Roberta remarked cryptically, and bustled off to her room, with Mrs. Ashley close behind.

The food was every bit as good as Sir Nicholas had promised, and by the time the last covers had been removed and the sweet wine drunk, there was a general feeling of good humor between them. Even Mrs. Ashley had unbent and had shown a remarkable friendliness toward Sir Nicholas.

If she only knew the truth of it, Roberta thought as they made their way from the private dining room to their respective bedrooms, she would be acting quite differently towards him. But it suited her plan for Mrs. Ashley to behave that way, for it would help lull Sir Nicholas into a false sense of security.

There was a long public passageway to negotiate between the dining room and the stairs, and as Roberta had been the one to open the door, she was, in effect, leading the party to bed. She passed one room whose door was slightly ajar, and with casual curiosity peeped in. Several men were seated around a large oval table, and she could see someone's hand dealing cards.

"It would appear that it is not only the food that attracts people here," she remarked as Sir Nicholas joined her. "Do they play for very high stakes?"

"Sometimes," he answered as he closed the door. "I have seen men lose large fortunes at that table."

Roberta shook her head in bafflement. "I have never understood what drives men to gamble all on the turn of a card."

"Women do as well," Sir Nicholas returned with a grin, although with his falsely aged face it looked more like a grimace. "There was one in particular, I remember—don't turn now," he continued us he hunched his shoulders slightly; "the comte is coming up behind you—disgusting performance, Roberta," he said, his voice rising angrily, "and one I wish you had witnessed. It would have taught you a lesson."

"Quite so, Papa," she said blithely, taking a few steps toward Sir Nicholas's right side. "Only, as I have never been tempted to gamble, I am at a loss to understand quite what lesson I would have learned by seeing this woman lose a fortune."

"That's not the point, Roberta," he grumbled as he leaned further over his cane. "You never know when temptation will come your way."

Mrs. Ashley looked curiously at the two of them and shrugged her shoulders. She had seen the stranger approaching and assumed they were enacting the scene for his benefit. Filled as she was with several glasses of wine, she decided to add further credence to their performance.

"Come, come, Roberta," she chided. "Leave your father in peace. You know you shouldn't agitate him just before bedtime." She brushed past them, tut-tutting, and continued past the comte, raising her eyebrows in seeming exasperation. "I never knew a more argumentative family," she sighed mournfully, and mounted the stairs. She thought she had seen the man nod in sympathy, and as she let herself into her bedroom, she felt well pleased by her performance.

"With your cheeseparing ways, Papa," Roberta continued crossly, "even if temptation did cross my path, I wouldn't have the means to be more than a bystander. Anyway, Ashley is quite right. You mustn't work yourself up into such a state so late in the evening. I'll see you to your door. Williams will be there to help you undress." She turned and started in surprise as the comte stepped in front of her. "You!" she gasped. "Ahem! Good evening. I had not expected to see you again."

The comte smiled, but Roberta noticed that his eyes remained hard and cold. "Mademoiselle Rushforth," he said as he took her hand and kissed it, "I hope you have forgiven me."

"Roberta!" Sir Nicholas snapped. "Who is this man? Why is he fondling you in such a fashion?"

The comte seemed unmoved by Sir Nicholas's questions, but Roberta, looking utterly adorable in her apparent confusion, quickly withdrew her hand. "It's—it's the gentleman I met on the boat," she said, and then, grinning sheepishly at the comte, added, "Please excuse Papa. He's an advocate of plain speaking, which sometimes can be quite embarrassing."

The comte bowed. "Then I will not add to your distress, mademoiselle. I bid you good night and hope that I will have the pleasure of meeting you again in London." He retreated up the passageway and watched through narrowed eyes as Roberta and Sir Nicholas made their way up the stairs. When they were finally out of sight, he snapped his fingers and a liveried servant appeared. "Find out where this Mlle. Rushforth resides," he commanded, and without a backward glance, pushed open the door to the gaming room and took his place at the table.

"What has he done that forces him to ask for your forgiveness?" Sir Nicholas demanded abruptly when he deemed that they were safely out of the comte's hearing.

Roberta blushed and looked to the floor. "I . . . ah . . . that really is none of your business," she answered, "but if it interests you, he tried to kiss me."

"Did he, by George!" Sir Nicholas exclaimed. "He must be very taken by you, Miss Rushforth, for I have never known him to indulge in such an unlikely flirtation before. Unless, of course, you encouraged him."

"Encouraged him!" Roberta sputtered, recalling how revolted she had felt by the comte's wet kiss. "How dare you even insinuate such a thing!"

Sir Nicholas laughed, but without mirth. "My apologies. I spoke without thinking. However, I beg you, please heed my warnings. He is a dangerous man to cross."

"I thank you for reminding me of that fact," she responded coldly. "And if anything untoward happens to me, I will not forget that you were the one responsible for my meeting him." She lifted her head arrogantly and entered her room, slamming the door hard behind her. "How dare he be so patronizing!" she fumed. "And so free with his advice?" It was about time someone exposed him for what he was, and it would be her pleasure to do so.

She undressed quickly and, tossing her clothes and her copy of the coded list haphazardly onto a chair, climbed wearily into bed. She thought sleep would elude her, but within seconds, her eyelids closed. As sleep overtook her, she remembered that she hadn't returned the paper to Sir Nicholas.

It was a dream, the recurring dream: she was being waltzed around the beeswaxed floor of Almack's by Stephen. She was only vaguely aware of the envious glances leveled at them by those young ladies who were not permitted to stand up for such an intimate dance, for her entire being was thrilling to Stephen's touch. They moved as one, swaying gracefully in perfect time to the music. Round and round they went, dipping, swirling, turning tirelessly.

Even so, her heart was heavy. There would be no tomorrow for her. After tonight, when she had told him that she wouldn't marry him, it would all be over, and she would never see him again.

She studied his face with tear-clouded eyes, etching every line in her mind. His eyes were half closed, and he smiled down at her lazily. She felt his arms tighten about her, and in a moment of total abandonment, she pressed herself closer to him.

"Happy, my darling girl?" he asked, his lips against her ear.

"Yes, yes," she cried incoherently. "I don't want this dance to end, ever."

But it did end, and it was with great reluctance that they parted and went in search of some liquid refreshment.

"Follow me," Stephen whispered after he had procured two glasses of lemonade, and in a trancelike state she did. He led her to a sparsely furnished antechamber and closed the door quietly. He placed the glasses on a small table and strode over to her. They looked at each other wordlessly, and then he caught her in an embrace. He kissed her on both eyes, her nose, her throat, and finally allowed his mouth to touch hers. She clung to him, momentarily forgetting what she had resolved to do, and allowed his tongue to part her lips. A wonderfully warm sensation coursed through her body. It came to an abrupt end when a fit of coughing overtook her.

"Are you all right, my darling?" he asked, concerned.

She pulled away from him and sat down. She was trembling from head to toe as she shook her head. "I cannot see you again, Stephen, ever," she whispered.

She moved restlessly in her sleep and brought a hand to her face as though to ward off something unpleasant. A faint noise penetrated her half-conscious state, and in a trice she was awake, the dream forgotten. She lay still, letting the silence of the night wash over her, and was finally rewarded by hearing someone move stealthily across the carpet. She had no idea of that person's direction or intent, but she feared it was the comte.

A dangerous man, Sir Nicholas had warned, used to taking what he wanted. Well, the comte had made no secret of the fact that he desired her, and she was equally determined not to be taken.

In one swift movement calculated to surprise the intruder, she reached out for the flint and candle that reposed on her bed table and kindled the wick. She sat up and held the feeble light aloft in both hands and moved it in an unsteady arc about the room. The flickering flame danced, creating shadows within shadows, and she was forced to wonder whether or not she had imagined any noise at all.

Slowly, she put the candle down on the commode and

sank back against the pillows, her breathing irregular. She stared first at the door, and then at the wardrobe that held her traveling gown at the far end of the room. She squinted, thinking at first that it was a trick of the light that produced the soft bulge to the side of the wardrobe, and then sat upright, rigid with fear, as the bulge moved.

"Papa?" she questioned, her voice no more than a whimper.

The bulge took shape as it detached itself from its hiding place, and Roberta, whose eyes were now accustomed to the half-light, could see that her second guess had been correct.

"Sir Nicholas!"

"And I had so hoped, Miss Rushforth, that I wouldn't disturb your sleep," he mocked, making her a half-bow.

"What on earth are you doing in my room at this time of night?" she gasped. "I demand an explanation for this unwarranted intrusion." She grabbed the bedclothes and held them high to her chin.

"Claiming my property," Sir Nicholas answered smoothly. "I believe you took a piece of paper from my cabin last night, and I want it back."

"You talk in riddles," she said defiantly.

"I don't mean to be obtuse," he answered as he moved closer to her bed.

"I will scream if you come any closer," Roberta warned him. "I think you had better go before I call for help."

His answer was to step right up to her. She watched his catlike movements in fascination and was taken completely by surprise when he bent down and brushed her lips with his.

"How dare you!" she exclaimed angrily, and brought a hand across his cheek in a resounding smack, heedless of the fact that her action had caused the bedclothes to slip to her waist.

"My dear Miss Rushforth, I have no intention of leaving this room without that piece of paper." He sat down beside her and twirled one of her short curls around his index finger. "Just tell me where you have hidden it, and I will leave you in peace."

As he spoke, his hand moved from her hair to her shoulder and gripped it with an intensity that hurt.

"Get out of my room, Sir Nicholas, before I scream," she hissed, struggling vainly to free herself.

He brought his face within an inch of hers and grinned. "I wouldn't do that if I were you, Miss Rushforth," he replied amiably, leaving no doubt in her mind that he was in full control of the situation. "You are in an extremely vulnerable position."

Her reflexes felt numb, except for the pounding of her heart, which she couldn't control. She tried to sink back again to her pillow, but his hand held her firm.

"Now tell me where it is, and I will leave you in peace."

"In the pocket of the dress in the wardrobe," she said wildly. "Take it and go!"

She looked away, afraid that he would ask her why she had taken it, that he would guess she had made a copy. He didn't, though, and she breathed a sigh of relief when he relinquished his hold of her. He rose and stood towering over her for several seconds, his shadow dancing on the walls in the candlelight. Her nerves felt frayed; she opened her mouth to scream, but no sound came. "It was very foolish of you to take that," he said. "What did you hope to gain except my attention?"

Without waiting for an answer, he picked up the candle and walked over to the wardrobe. Then, with his injured arm, he gingerly prised open the door and fumbled awkwardly with her dress until he finally found what he was looking for. He grunted in satisfaction and scanned it quickly, then placed it in his pocket.

"Thank you for your cooperation, Miss Rushforth," he said, a smile playing at the corners of his mouth. "I am sorry if I have caused you any discomfort."

She sat, transfixed, as he allowed his gaze to wander over her. Then, without warning, he blew the candle out. Then, and only then, did she sink back.

"I would advise you to lock the door behind me, Miss Rushforth," he said, his voice penetrating the darkness like the crack of a whip. "Your lack of modesty will, of a certainty, land you in a great deal of trouble."

She heard him returning the candlestick to the commode, and in a fit of ungovernable rage, she reached behind her for a pillow. She hurled it at him with all her might, but he was out of the door before it landed. She relit the candle to see what had caused his final comment, and blushed. The coverlet had slipped right down to her waist, and beneath her transparent gown, her breasts were clearly visible.

"Damn you, Sir Nicholas," she muttered in most unlady-like tones. "You are going to pay dearly for this."

chapter 7

THE FINAL STAGE of the journey was concluded in silence.
Mrs. Ashley, who felt some resentment that no one had
acknowledged her efforts to hoodwink the stranger the previous night, could not but notice the deliberate rudeness
Roberta displayed toward Sir Nicholas. She was perplexed
by Roberta's attitude, for she had never before seen her
charge act in such a way.

She stole a look at Sir Nicholas, who appeared to be
composed, almost to the point of boredom. Roberta, on the
other hand, looked angrier than a wet hen. Mrs. Ashley
shrugged and decided to ask Roberta what it was all about,
when they were alone.

This, however, didn't occur until long after they had
reached Lord Bromley's house in Grosvenor Square. After
such a long absence, all the servants had lined up to welcome
Roberta home. The house steward, with his prepared
speech, managed to put a smile on Roberta's face, Mrs.
Ashley was pleased to note. Perhaps afterward would be a
good time to question her charge. Unfortunately, the house-
keeper, a motherly soul, whisked Roberta away before Mrs.
Ashley could even beg a private word, and she felt exceedingly annoyed.

By late afternoon, though, when the excitement of their
arrival had died down and the household staff had resumed
its normal duties, Mrs. Ashley sent word to Roberta to come
and join her for a cup of tea.

"I received the distinct impression this morning that you
were annoyed with Sir Nicholas over something," she said
without preamble when Roberta eventually joined her.

"Annoyed, Ashley?" Roberta queried with a laugh. "No, annoyed is to be provoked, and I refuse to acknowledge that someone of Sir Nicholas's color can affect me so. I have merely followed your lead, Ashley, dear, and have taken him in dislike. I cannot think why I let myself be persuaded to help him, and feel that I cannot apologize to you sufficiently for not heeding your initial advice."

"But what happened? You both seemed at ease with each other over dinner last night. Indeed, I was quite charmed by his exceedingly gracious manner myself, and revised my earlier opinion of him, despite the circumstances that necessitated his escape from France."

"I have nothing further to say on that particular topic, Ashley, until I have spoken to my uncle," Roberta replied firmly. "Unfortunately, Perkins, Uncle's new secretary, has informed me he will be out of town until next week."

Mrs. Ashley sighed unhappily. She knew better than to argue. Roberta sighed as well, but hers was one of frustration. She had simply not expected that Lord Bromley would be anywhere but London, and when she had learned he was in the north of England, she had vented the exasperation she had felt on the unfortunate Mr. Perkins. Now there was nothing left for her to do but while away the days until he returned, and hope that Sir Nicholas would not vanish in the meantime.

She paid scant attention to Mrs. Ashley as she sipped the hot tea, for she was caught up in forming a plan that would enable her to keep an eye on Sir Nicholas. There had to be a way that would not arouse his suspicions.

"Dear Ashley, what a bore I am," she exclaimed when she realized her companion had been talking. "Here I am, rapt in my own maudlin reflections and not paying the slightest heed to what you are saying. Forgive me, please."

"Think nothing of it, Roberta. I was merely reproaching myself for not showing a greater understanding of your mood. You must be in a turmoil about meeting Mr. Davenport again." She broke off, as if afraid she had said too much.

Roberta, startled by this deduction, averted her gaze. Two days ago she would have agreed, but now she had something far more worrisome with which to concern herself. She looked out of the window and absentmindedly watched the wind ripple the leaves of the weeping pear tree.

"It will not be easy," she conceded. "People are bound to gossip, but . . ." She paused as the final solution to her dilemma, how to keep Sir Nicholas at her side, came to her.

"Yes?" Mrs. Ashley asked impatiently.

"I don't want to shock you by the forwardness of my suggestion, but I thought to enlist Sir Nicholas's aid. In a way, you could say I would be asking him to repay the debt he owes us."

"Whatever do you have in mind?"

"I'm going to ask him if he will squire me about Town. Just until I'm settled in Society, you understand. But you must see that if it appears I have a beau dangling after me, any gossip attendant to my past association with Stephen will be short-lived." Roberta could see that her idea both appalled and intrigued Mrs. Ashley, and she pressed her advantage. "I didn't tell you before, for fear of upsetting you, but I met the comte on the boat, and he was the man at the inn last night. He intimated then that he would try to see me in London."

"Oh, Lordy me!" Mrs. Ashley moaned. "How perfectly horrendous. Why on earth did Lord Bromley have to choose this week to absent himself?"

"Then do you agree with me that if Sir Nicholas will consent to my scheme, he will provide the perfect, double-edged protection we need until my uncle returns?"

Mrs. Ashley nodded. "I will send him a card immediately, asking him to call on me first thing in the morning. Do we know where he is staying? No matter," she continued, all aflutter in the wake of Roberta's disclosure. "Williams will know, for he took him home after he delivered us safely."

Roberta smiled sweetly. She was happy to let Mrs. Ashley take charge. Somehow she knew her preposterous suggestion would not seem so outrageous to Sir Nicholas if it were put forward by someone else. Also, she was of the opinion that Sir Nicholas would find a way to refuse her request, but he wouldn't treat Mrs. Ashley in the insolent fashion with which he would treat her.

* * *

Sir Nicholas's lodgings, spartan when compared to Lord Bromley's luxuriously appointed town house, suited his present needs to perfection. He seldom spent more than two nights of any week there, yet it was safe enough to house the documents and papers that were necessary for his work. He kept two servants: Jenkins, a butler, who doubled as a groom, and Davids, a valet, who was also his chef. Both men he regarded as faithful watchdogs, and he trusted them implicitly.

When the mood for a grander style of living came upon him, he took himself off to Stanway, his estate near Tewkesbury. Whenever he stayed at Stanway, Sir Nicholas was content to accept the unsophisticated entertainment offered by the local gentry, for it provided a pleasing contrast to the life his work forced him to lead in London. For the moment, though, he was content to be in Town.

After Williams had set him down in Albemarle Street, he had been whisked away by his two servants and had allowed them to tend his wound. It pleased him to discover it wasn't as serious as he had first suspected. He had refused to go to bed. Instead, he ordered Jenkins to stoke up the fire in his study and asked Davids to prepare him a tempting meal. He was hungry, but he had a lot of work to do. Then, when he was alone, he pulled out the papers he had brought with him from France and spread them out on his desk.

By early evening, his eyes had tired from studying the hieroglyphics, and he pushed the papers to one side. He stood up and stretched, letting out a loud oath when he jammed his injured shoulder. He was rubbing it ruefully when Jenkins entered.

"Is dinner ready?" Sir Nicholas asked, suddenly remembering his hunger.

"In twenty minutes, my lord," Jenkins replied as he held out a silver salver on which reposed a thick ivory vellum envelope. "This came for you an hour ago."

Sir Nicholas took the envelope and slit it open slowly. He scanned the spidery writing and then whistled in surprise.

"Will that be all, Sir Nicholas?" Jenkins inquired. "I told the messenger not to wait and that we would send a reply if it was necessary."

"No, there is no need for a reply. My presence at Grosvenor Square at eleven tomorrow morning will be answer enough."

"Lord Bromley?" Jenkins exclaimed in surprise.

"No; Roberta, his niece, or should I say his niece's companion, Mrs. Ashley, requests the dubious pleasure of my company."

"I see, Sir Nicholas," Jenkins said, his face resuming its impassive expression. "I didn't think Lord Bromley had returned from Mr. Lambert's funeral."

"It's no good trying to pump any answers out of me," Sir Nicholas said with a laugh, "for I must confess I have no idea what this note means. When I parted company from the two ladies this morning, I thought I had seen the last of them. I suspect Miss Rushforth is behind this summons, though, and *that* I find intriguing."

"Will you be taking Davids with you?"

Sir Nicholas shook his head. "I'll go on foot. I hardly think I need any protection from Mrs. Ashley."

"But the comte. Will he not be looking for you?"

Sir Nicholas arched an eyebrow disdainfully, giving Jenkins the clear impression he was not concerned over that possibility. "I can hardly prevent him from walking the streets of London, can I, Jenkins? He has no proof that it was I he saw leaving his chateau, so I think it unlikely he will accost me in public."

"Your injury?" Jenkins interposed.

"Unless he is able to strip me, he will never see it. Look," he continued as he rotated his arm slowly, "the stiffness has almost disappeared. In another day or two, I will be as good as new. Now tell Davids I am ready to eat."

The matter was closed, as far as he was concerned, and he watched in some amusement as Jenkins, with an unhappy sigh, withdrew.

Roberta watched the traffic in Grosvenor Square from the vantage point of her bedroom window, waiting the arrival of Sir Nicholas. Finally, she saw him enter the square on foot. He was wearing an expertly tailored cloak that hugged his shoulders like a glove, and his high beaver hat was pulled low over his forehead. The cloak protected him to a nicety against the cool wind, and the hat hid his face.

There was only one way of identifying him—by his long, purposeful stride.

The sound of the door knocker echoed up the stairs. Roberta glanced at herself in the mirror and laughed at her image. The lace cap atop her curls, which she was wearing despite Mrs. Ashley's entreaties, looked faintly ridiculous. Her morning dress of gray silk was buttoned high to her neck, and the long sleeves were edged in white. Matching gray slippers on her dainty feet peeked out beneath the folds of the gathered skirt, and about her waist she had tied a twisted rope belt of white silk. She wanted to appear demure, and she had succeeded admirably.

She heard the hall clock chime the quarter hour and began to make her way downstairs. Mrs. Ashley had suggested she present herself in the green sitting room twenty minutes after Sir Nicholas's arrival, deeming it sufficient time in which to persuade him to help them.

Roberta tapped lightly on the door and walked in. Avoiding looking directly at Sir Nicholas, she hesitated and waited for Mrs. Ashley to drop a handkerchief to the floor. It was their prearranged signal that Mrs. Ashley had been successful in her endeavors. Only when Roberta saw it flutter down did she acknowledge his presence.

"Sir Nicholas," she exclaimed, feigning a haughty surprise. "I had not expected to see you again so soon."

"Your servant, Miss Rushforth," he replied. He paused briefly before bowing over her hand, giving her plenty of time to see his amused expression. He quite obviously didn't believe she was surprised, but she didn't care.

"How is your shoulder?" she inquired coldly. "I trust you haven't suffered any further setbacks."

"None at all, Miss Rushforth. I am quite on the mend, as you can see."

Roberta looked at him quizzically, determined to play her part to the end. She would never give him the pleasure of confirming his suspicions that she had been behind Mrs. Ashley's summons. "I am sorry I was not here to receive you. I trust Mrs. Ashley has kept you entertained?"

"But I'm here at her urging," he answered. "She had rather an unusual request to make of me," he added quickly before Roberta had time to feign any further surprise.

"Is this correct, Ashley?" she queried.

Mrs. Ashley nodded and shifted uncomfortably in her chair. She was filled with misgivings, for Sir Nicholas's acceptance of her proposal had been too quick. He had neither pressed for any explanations about Roberta's past connection with Stephen Davenport nor made any comment when she had voiced her fears about the comte's promise to see Roberta in London. In fact, now that she thought on it, she felt he had been far too acquiescent to her outrageous proposal.

Roberta, misinterpreting her silence, glanced toward Sir Nicholas for an explanation. "What was this request, Sir Nicholas?"

"Mrs. Ashley, with every justification, is concerned lest the comte acts on the promise he made, to visit you in London."

"And?" Roberta demanded.

"She has asked me to escort you to a few social functions and let it appear I'm dangling after you, in an effort to discourage him."

"What!" Roberta expostulated, trying vainly to sound shocked. "How—how utterly preposterous. I hope you refused."

"On the contrary, Miss Rushforth, I have accepted the challenge. Only, I hasten to add, until the comte returns to France. I'm aware of how trying you find my company, and wouldn't presume to inflict myself on you after the threat posed by the comte's presence has been removed."

"How could you do such a thing without consulting me, Ashley?" Roberta asked, ignoring Sir Nicholas. "I find it too embarrassing for words."

"I thought it for the best, Roberta," Mrs. Ashley replied nervously. "If Lord Bromley had been here, I wouldn't have resorted to such a tack. As matters stand, I didn't know how else to protect you."

"I could stay at home," Roberta retorted, glaring at Mrs. Ashley. "I still quite understand if you want to change your mind, Sir Nicholas," she continued, "for I certainly wouldn't dream of holding you to such a promise. I don't think for one moment the comte will concern himself with me, should he appear in London. He probably has far more urgent matters to attend to, anyway."

"Even so, Miss Rushforth, in light of the confrontations

you had with him, I deem it a wise precaution to give you what protection I can."

Roberta shrugged in defeat. "I can't stop you from paying attention to me," she said, "but I don't have to encourage your advances."

"Indeed not, and I wouldn't expect you to," Sir Nicholas answered.

Mrs. Ashley looked at them uncertainly. There was an air of tension about them which she found perplexing. She cleared her throat. "I realize this arrangement is a trifle unorthodox, Roberta, but I hope we can all brush along without any unpleasantness."

"I don't see why not, Mrs. Ashley," Sir Nicholas said, smiling politely. "I shall do my utmost to act the part of a lovelorn calf, and Miss Rushforth will have to do her best to repel me."

Roberta, genuinely amused by the picture Sir Nicholas had painted of himself, threw back her head and laughed. "Now that you couch it in those terms," she said, "I'm all impatience to begin. Methinks I will enjoy my role after all."

"I thought you would," Sir Nicholas replied, "so let us not delay a moment before we begin this charade. I propose we three go to the theater tonight and let all of London see me paying court to you."

Roberta glanced at Mrs. Ashley to see if she had any objections, and then nodded her approval. "Mrs. Ashley and I will use Lord Bromley's box at the Drury Lane Theatre, and perhaps you can visit us in the first intermission. The mere fact that I receive you will give the gossips something to ponder."

"It will be my pleasure," Sir Nicholas murmured with a grin.

"No doubt at my expense," Roberta snapped, but apparently he didn't hear, for he was bowing over Mrs. Ashley's hand and bidding her good day.

He was gone before Roberta had time to summon the butler, and she felt an irritation that only Sir Nicholas seemed capable of causing. It was his self-assured air. Nothing seemed to overset him.

"If he thinks to use me as a passport to enter the upper

echelons of Society," she said after the door had closed behind him, "he is in for a rude awakening."

"He doesn't need that, Roberta," Mrs. Ashley responded, her hands fluttering nervously about her bodice. "I looked him up in DeBrett. He's there already. He inherited his estates from the Earl of Wemyss and uses Stanway as his country home."

"Then how is it we have never met him before? Has he been a recluse until now?"

"I don't know, Roberta," Mrs. Ashley said thoughtfully.

"You were quite right in your judgment of him, Ashley. He really is too exasperating."

Mrs. Ashley shook her head, oblivious to Roberta's words. "Even so," she continued, still deep in thought, "I can't imagine how anyone who appears as eligible as Sir Nicholas has managed to escape the Marriage Mart. There must be some scandal attached to his name that we haven't heard of. Or it could be that he has purposely shunned Society. There are men, you know, who actively dislike women."

"But not Sir Nicholas," Roberta said, thinking of the experienced way he had pinned her to her bed. "Anyway, I'm not going to worry. If he has any faults, we will hear them all tomorrow, for after my friends and acquaintances see me tonight, they will come flocking here on the pretext of welcoming me home, whereas we both know that in reality, they will be coming to divulge all."

"Such cynicism doesn't suit you, Roberta," Mrs. Ashley said reprovingly. "Your friends will come out of genuine regard for you, and the rest you don't have to receive."

"What! And miss the opportunity to hear what is being said about my latest beau?" Roberta mocked. "I will welcome anyone who calls." And perhaps, she added to herself, she would be able to find out a little more about Sir Nicholas and who he really was.

chapter 8

UNFORTUNATELY, ROBERTA WAS doomed to disappointment. None of her visitors the next day was able to add to her knowledge of Sir Nicholas.

It wasn't that there was any mystery surrounding him, for everyone seemed to know of his connection to the late Earl of Wemyss, and his preference for country living. According to Sally Jersey, who was one of the first callers that day, he had been about London for more years than she cared to remember, but he had never shown any inclination to indulge himself in the pleasure offered by mothers with eligible daughters. His preference, she had stated, was for more sophisitcated entertainment. This, Roberta had interpreted, meant that he would rather spend his time with his mistress than mixing with the fashionable crowd.

No wonder she had never heard of him! she thought after the last morning visitor had departed. He had obviously gone to great lengths to make it appear as though he led a very ordinary life.

These reflections caused her to think of the copy of the list she had in her possession, and without more ado she took herself off to her own private sitting room to study it. She sat down at her writing desk and scrutinized the jumble of letters. It was most discouraging, however, for it was akin to reading a foreign language.

There had to be a key that would unravel the code, but she was blessed if she could fathom it. It galled her to realize that even now Sir Nicholas was making sense of the very same list while she doodled idly on a fresh sheet of paper. She rearranged the first set of letters, as she had done countless times before when trying to work out an anagram.

A discreet knock on the door caused her to shove her work into a drawer, and she moved away from her desk before the butler entered. He was carrying two floral arrangements, and she directed him to deposit them both on the small end table by the sofa.

When he had departed, she looked for the cards. The smaller bouquet, a delightful collection of spring blooms, was from Sir Nicholas.

To commemorate your return to an English spring.
Until we meet tomorrow at Lady Sefton's soirée. N.

His bold handwriting took up the entire card.

The second display was composed of hothouse flowers, not at all to her liking. She pulled the card from the green leaves and stood motionless as she recognized the small, almost indecipherable, letters.

"Stephen," she whispered.

She forced herself to open the envelope but sat down before she read the note. The moment of their meeting couldn't be far away if he knew she was in Town. The thought caused her knees to shake uncontrollably. She read the letter through a haze of tears and then let it fall to the carpet as she stared into middle distance, trying vainly to regain her composure.

Roberta, my dear. You can imagine my surprise and joy when I saw you enter Lord Bromley's box last night, looking as ethereal as I remembered you from our last meeting. I had not heard that you were back in Town. There is so much I have to tell you, yet I know it would be unwise to seek you out publicly for any length of time. If, perchance, you intend to be present at Lady Sefton's gathering tomorrow night, and feel able to grant me my heart's desire of a private interview, I beg that you pin two of these orchirds to your dress. It will be the only sign I need to know that you will receive me when I call at Grosvenor Square. As always, Stephen.

All thoughts of Sir Nicholas and the list were relegated to the back of Roberta's mind as she tried to resolve the best course to follow. Then, with a swiftness that characterized most of her decisions, she decided to wear the orchids. She could not abide the idea of airing her emotions in public, and Stephen had unwittingly provided the best solution to his particular problem. She would be able to acknowledge him with a nod at Lady Sefton's, thereby robbing the ardent gossips of talk.

Roberta's reentry into Society was a marked success. She had chosen her gown carefully, conscious that she would be the center of attraction, for the Season was still young and the crowds thin. Her presence, her good looks and her elegant gown were noted and remarked on by those dowagers who didn't have daughters of marrying age, and they welcomed her into their circle happily.

But the several matrons who were unfortunate enough to have young, unmarried daughters were overheard to comment that Roberta Rushforth had become a turf-hunter, which was only to be expected, in view of her advancing years.

Sir Nicholas, who happened to be standing behind two hard-faced matrons, could not but help hear their stinging remarks. It was with the utmost difficulty that he restrained himself from delivering them a piece of his mind.

He looked across to Roberta, who was by now surrounded by many of her old friends, and laughed. A minx would have been a more apt description for her, but with her own vast inheritance and her independent spirit, she could never be a turf-hunter. He watched with interest as a tall, broad-shouldered individual entered the ballroom. For a moment, Sir Nicholas was convinced all conversation ceased as everyone stared, first at the man and then at Roberta. But when Roberta acknowledged the stranger with a cool nod, the noise rose to its former high pitch, and Sir Nicholas was convinced he had been mistaken. It was only when he heard someone say, "It's Stephen Davenport, isn't it?" that he realized this was the moment, at least according to Mrs. Ashley, Roberta had been dreading most of all.

"She handled herself remarkably well," he said to Mrs.

Ashley a little while later, "and, if I'm not mistaken, has disappointed quite a few people."

"I'm inclined to agree with you, Sir Nicholas. I don't pretend to understand why some of my acquaintances feed off other people's weaknesses, but they do." She broke off in some agitation and put a nervous hand on Sir Nicholas's satin sleeve. "Is—is that who I think it is?" she whispered, nodding in the direction of the receiving line.

He nodded and smiled reassuringly at her. "Our friend the comte," he murmured. "What a busy person he is. Excuse me, I think I will try to penetrate the circle surrounding Miss Rushforth and be on hand when he advances."

"Please, please go, quickly." She propelled him toward Roberta and stood, bosom heaving in agitation, awaiting the inevitable confrontation.

Sir Nicholas managed to press his way to Roberta's side and claim her hand for the next dance before the comte had even finished greeting Lady Sefton. By the time the dance was over, Sir Nicholas had obviously primed Roberta, because she was able to greet the comte with remarkable equanimity when he approached her.

From her vantage point, Mrs. Ashley had noticed a slight stiffness about Sir Nicholas's injured arm while he had been dancing, but this seemed to disappear as he shook hands firmly with the comte. She only heard later from Roberta, as they were sipping a last cup of chocolate prior to going to bed, that the comte had deliberately caught Sir Nicholas's arm at the elbow and had pulled it quite savagely.

"I didn't realize what he was about, until it was too late," Roberta said, "but Sir Nicholas displayed remarkable restraint. He managed to extricate himself quite quickly, but I could see by his eyes that he was in considerable pain."

"Oh, dear! I do hope the comte doesn't do anything untoward," Mrs. Ashley murmured. "You don't think he suspects anything, do you?"

"Sir Nicholas is perfectly able to take care of himself," Roberta remarked dryly. "He neither encourages nor wants our sympathy." This remark was caused by the rebuff she had received from him when, following the comte's departure, she had inquired after his well-being. "By the way, he suggested a drive in Hyde Park tomorrow, but I declined.

I thought that to be seen with him three days in a row would be unseemly."

Mrs. Ashley nodded. "And what of Mr. Davenport? I was pleased to see how you managed to avoid a direct confrontation with him."

Roberta glanced down at the orchids, now slightly wilted, still pinned to her dress. "If our future meetings can be so innocuous, then I, too, will be pleased. I expect there were many disappointed people, though," she added with a chuckle. "I'm certain many were hoping for something more dramatic. His wife seemed very pleasant, didn't you think?"

"Lady Anita, by all accounts, conducts herself admirably. She turns a blind eye to his infidelities and refuses to hear a word said against him."

"Stephen wouldn't behave like that," Roberta exclaimed in shocked tones. "I know you have never liked him, Ashley, but there is no need to relate malicious gossip."

Mrs. Ashley snapped her mouth closed in a thin line, as if to prevent herself from saying anything she would later regret, and sighed unhappily.

"We'll never see eye to eye on him," Roberta said in an effort to placate her, "so please don't let's argue about it any more."

"I'll try, Roberta, I'll try. However, I won't sit by and see you make a cake of yourself over some fortune hunter. I may be repeating gossip, but I had no intention of being malicious. There was one hard fact I learned tonight that I feel compelled to tell you about. Your Mr. Davenport was involved in a card game several months ago and dropped five thousand guineas to Sir George Beattie. At the end of the evening, when all the chits had been accounted for, Mr. Davenport scandalized the gathering by informing Sir George that as soon as he had prised the money from his wife, he would repay the debt."

Although Roberta found this news disturbing, she adamantly refused to be swayed in her judgment of Stephen. "He may have been under the influence of drink *if* he actually used those words, or maybe Sir George misunderstood. Please, Ashley, don't say any more tonight."

"Very well, Roberta," Mrs. Ashley replied. "I'll do my best in the future to ignore all the things I hear about him."

She rose and left the room like a galleon in full sail, obviously annoyed by Roberta's stubbornness on the subject of Stephen Davenport.

It was some time after eleven the next day before Roberta, at the same window from which she had watched for Sir Nicholas a few days earlier, saw Stephen enter Grosvenor Square. With a fine disregard for decorum, she flew down the stairs and arrived at the front door before the knocker had even sounded. She dismissed the footman with an airy wave and opened the massive portal just as Stephen was mounting the last step. Her heart fluttered as he smiled down at her.

Without a word, she beckoned him in and led him to the nearest sitting room. It was a small, intimate antechamber for waiting visitors. While he closed the door, she moved across the blue carpet to the far side in an effort to put as much space between them as possible. She was afraid to touch him, or allow him to touch her, lest she lose control of herself altogether.

They stood thus, staring across at each other, until Stephen finally made her a bow. "My dear, dear Roberta, how are you?"

His deep, resonant voice was exactly as she remembered it. Even so, she was unprepared for the effect it had on her. "Well . . . well," she choked. "And you?"

He grimaced and shrugged. "Older and wiser, some people tell me, but today I feel as green as I did my first day at Eton. Oh, Roberta! If you only knew how I have regretted allowing you to send me away. A day hasn't passed when I haven't chastised myself for believing the nonsense you gave me about Lord Bromley refusing to countenance our marriage. When I finally discovered the truth, it was too late. You were in Switzerland, and I was married. Why, why did you do such a thing?"

Roberta, totally unprepared for this outburst, turned away quickly. She had remembered Stephen for his strength, not for the self-pity he was now displaying.

"I thought it best, under the circumstances," she whispered. "I had been informed by four prominent specialists that I would be an invalid for the rest of my life. Knowing that, I couldn't marry you. It wouldn't have been fair."

"You didn't trust me enough, did you? Perhaps you even thought that if I knew, I wouldn't stand by you. Was that it?" His voice was accusing, and it pierced Roberta's heart liks a sharp knife.

"No, no, Stephen," she cried. "I was certain you would insist on standing by me. That is why I lied to you. I refused to give you the opportunity to act nobly, because I was afraid you would live to regret it."

"And instead I have the rest of my life to regret my hasty marriage to Anita."

He sounded bitter now, and Roberta looked at him in surprise. For the first time she saw the lines of discontent and dissipation on his face. Was she responsible for this dreadful change in him? she wondered bleakly.

"You don't know what it's like, Roberta," he continued, seemingly unaware of her troubled expression. "Anita keeps me on such a tight rein. She treats me like a halfling, rather than a man. She uses the fact that she has a fortune to make me toe the line. It's—it's insufferable!"

"She doesn't appear to me to be such a harridan," Roberta exclaimed involuntarily. "I received the impression last night that she was a warm, soft person."

He ground his fist into the palm of his other hand impatiently. "Appearances can sometimes be deceptive. She's hard and demanding when we are alone." He broke off. "Bu I didn't come here to speak of her, Roberta. I want to talk about us." He caught her unresisting hands in his. "I want to hear you say that you still care for me as I care for you. That you want to recapture those halcyon days we used to enjoy. I want you to agree to see me alone, as often as you can."

Roberta stared up at him uncomprehendingly before disengaging her hands. "I don't think you know what you are suggesting," she said in a low voice.

"My little innocent darling," he murmured in a voice that was meant to caress her. "I need you so desperately, in a way that only a man who loves a woman with all his heart could. I want you to be my mistress."

Roberta's hands fluttered to her face, but even they

couldn't hide her shocked expression.

"I've upset you, haven't I?" he said. "My suggestion is too bold. You need time to consider it?"

"No, Stephen. Please don't say anything more. I could never agree to such a thing. It goes against every value I've ever believed in. I can't pretend that I've not imagined what it would be like to be in your arms. But I suppose I have come to realize it can never be."

"Then why did you wear my orchids last night? You must have known what you were implying, surely?"

Roberta shook her head. "I didn't. I just knew I wanted to see you again. I didn't think beyond that."

"Well, you've seen me again. Now what?" he demanded belligerently.

"Nothing," she countered helplessly. "I mean, I don't know."

"You're disappointed in me, aren't you?" he answered, the angry note back in his voice. "Because I spoke like a man and expressed my need for you, you take offense. Fool that I was. I expected you to be different. I had convinced myself you would understand. But the reality is that you're no different, no more understanding, than any other woman of my acquaintance. Like all other females, you put out lures to snare a man and then recoil as the trap is sprung."

Roberta stared at him, aghast. Suddenly all the hints that Mrs. Ashley had dropped about Stephen's character came pouring back. She stiffened.

"Are you any better, Stephen?" she asked. "You use your wife's wealth to pursue your own pleasure, but you're not loyal to her. You demand loyalty and perfection in others, but you seem incapable of living up to those standards yourself."

"What do you mean?" he asked.

"I'm referring to a particular game of cards you had with Sir George Beattie, when you lost a considerable sum of money. You had some very unkind words to say about your wife on that occasion."

"Oh, that!" he retorted. "I spoke no less than the truth. Anita is very tight when it comes to parting with money. But that will change in a few years, when the control of her fortune passes to me. If that damned father of hers hadn't tied up the bulk of it until she had reached the age of thirty, I would be in control of it now."

"In the circumstances, it would appear to have been a wise move," she murmured.

"So George thought I was offensive, did he?" Stephen continued. "Well, your friend didn't. He was most sympathetic when the game was over. He even offered to lend me the ready himself."

"My friend?" Roberta queried, genuinely bewildered by the turn the conversation had taken.

"The Frenchman who was fawning over you last night."

"The comte?" she said in astonishment. "Why, I hardly know the man. And from what I do know of him, I'm surprised to hear of his generosity."

Stephen laughed. "Everything has its price, my darling," he remarked. "His was an introduction to various members of my club. Influential people, I hasten to add."

"Whom did he mention?" Roberta asked, the shock she had felt at Stephen's outrageous proposal momentarily suppressed by curiosity.

"Mr. Lambert, for one, God rest his soul," Stephen replied, happy to see Roberta returning to her normal self again. "And Edmund Truscott."

"The Defense Minister's secretary?"

Stephen nodded. "Then there was Lacey Sigmore. And an up-and-coming politician, Wilfred Barns. Oh, I don't know! There were several more—not that it matters—but as far as I can recall, they were all connected to politics in one way or another. He's an ambitious man, the comte. Although why I'm wasting my time speaking of such things baffles me completely." He moved toward her again, his confidence returning. "Do you let me live in hope, Roberta?" he asked abruptly. "Will the day ever come when you will finally accept the inevitable?"

Roberta, dumbfounded by his insensitivity, was suddenly forced to wonder why she had spent so many months believing she was deeply in love with him. He simply wasn't the same person she remembered.

"Don't touch me, Stephen," she said with a calmness

that stopped him cold. "I will forget that we ever had this conversation, and I hope that you will do likewise. Now, if you will excuse me, there are a few chores that command my attention."

"You hypocritical little fool," he blustered. "You know you want me more than anything else in the world. Why do you deny yourself?"

Roberta surveyed him for a moment and then picked her way daintily to the door and turned to face him for the last time. "Until an hour ago, I would have agreed with your statement, Stephen. But now . . . the truth is that I no longer want you. By refusing your invitation to become your mistress, I'm not denying myself anything I want."

"You talk in riddles, Roberta," he fumed. "What has happened to make you change your mind?"

"Your attitude toward your wife," she responded quietly. "I think it reflects your general attitude toward all women, and I find it horrifying. Women, Stephen, are not creatures to be used. They are human beings with emotions and feelings every bit as complicated as those of men."

"Good heavens, Roberta, I'm not that insensitive. I have probably, in the heat of the moment, overstated my resentment toward my wife. But you must understand that in my joy at seeing you, I cast all caution to the winds."

"I don't think I misunderstood you at all, Stephen. How long would it be before you found me an encumbrance? And then what would you do? Discard me like a lame horse and continue with your life as though nothing had happened?"

"It wouldn't be like that, Roberta. I would never tire of you. Never."

"Really, Stephen? I don't believe that for one moment, and neither do you."

Before he could reply, she left the room and asked the hovering footman to see Stephen out. As she climbed the stairs to her bedroom, she couldn't quite believe she had been able to leave him so easily, with so little sorrow. Yet, for the first time since she had broken off her engagement, she felt free of the bonds holding her to him.

Perhaps when the mystery surrounding Sir Nicholas was

cleared up, and she had time to ponder exactly what it was that had triggered her final disgust of Stephen, she wouldn't feel quite so free.

But for the moment, she had no time for such reflections. Something Stephen had said had given her an idea as to how she could break the code of the list, and with single-minded determination, she hurried upstairs to study it.

chapter 9

THE MORNING AFTER Lady Sefton's gathering, a frustrated frown creased Sir Nicholas's brow, and with uncharacteristic sharpness, he cursed Davids roundly for neglecting to have sufficient hot water on hand for his bath.

His temper had been aroused by the comte's presence in London, and he knew that unless he was able to make sense very soon of the lists he had stolen, his bad mood would continue. Every day that passed without a solution meant the comte could continue to ingratiate himself into Society. And Sir Nicholas's temper had not been helped by Roberta's attitude. She had been far too pleasant toward the comte and now, on reflection, he suspected her behavior had been a deliberate ploy to encourage the dratted Frenchman's suit. She was playing a very dangerous game, and as yet, he couldn't fathom what she hoped to gain. Add to that the incident of the paper she had taken from his cabin. What did she want? Another mystery . . . and a disturbing one.

"Drat the girl," he murmured. "All this nonsense could have been avoided if Lord Bromley had been home when we arrived back from France."

"Sir Nicholas?" Davids ventured tentatively, wondering what on earth had caused Sir Nicholas to vent his spleen so early in the day. It made him uneasy to see his master so obviously out of sorts. "Sir Nicholas?" he repeated when he realized his master hadn't heard his first remark.

"Don't stand there looking at me as if I had just descended in a hot-air balloon," Sir Nicholas said irritably. "I was merely commenting to myself that Lord Bromley's absence from London was ill-timed."

"As was Mr. Lambert's death," Davids said solemnly. "Such a shock. So totally unexpected. To think he was here for dinner three weeks ago."

"Quite so," Sir Nicholas replied, and threw another crumpled stock onto the already large pile on the floor.

"Perhaps you would like me to fashion your necktie?" Davids asked. "Your shoulder must be tiring you by now."

"I'm perfectly capable of doing it myself, Davids. Oh, very well!" he added as his servant allowed an injured expression to cross his face. "Do what you can with this."

Davids deftly folded a clean stock and wrapped it about Sir Nicholas's neck. With a few expert moves, he produced a Windfall knot and stood back to admire his handiwork. "That should do it, Sir Nicholas," he commented in satisfaction. "Now, if you will just let me ease your arms into your jacket, your toilet will be complete."

"Damn your unfailing good humor," Sir Nicholas said with a smile. "You make it impossible for one to have the dods with any degree of enjoyment."

David's face brightened considerably at this, for it was a sure indication that Sir Nicholas's ill-disposition was coming to an end. "Will you be needing me again this morning?" he inquired.

"No, and I'll be dining out tonight. Take the rest of the day off and enjoy yourself. By the way, how is the young lady you were pursuing before I left for France?"

Davids looked down at the carpet and shuffled his large feet in embarrassment. "That would be Polly, Sir Nicholas. She can be quite contrary when she wants."

"Hanging out for a wedding band, is she?" Sir Nicholas chuckled, knowing his servant fancied himself a ladies' man.

David's embarrassment became acute. "She's indicated that is what she wants."

"Is that what you want?" Sir Nicholas asked.

"I'm not in a position even to consider such a state," Davids replied with a shake of his head. "And so I've told her several times already."

"Afraid I wouldn't countenance such a move, are you?"

"It wouldn't be right," Davids said stubbornly. "We never know from one day to the next where we'll be, do we? I could never ask anyone to share that sort of life."

Sir Nicholas looked at him thoughtfully for a moment. "You know, there would always be a permanent position for you at Stanway, Davids, if you decided you could not live without this Polly."

"And who would look after you, Sir Nicholas? I wouldn't trust anyone but myself or Jenkins."

"It wouldn't be easy to replace you, but it could be done. Don't, I beg you, allow a lifetime of happiness to elude you on my account. You will live to regret it and one day might place the blame for your unhappiness at my doorstep. Who knows," he added in an effort to erase David's doleful expression, "I might even retire when this assignment is over and done with. I fancy I'm getting a little too old for all this melodramatic work."

"If that happens, Sir Nicholas, then I might reconsider my situation." Davids smiled wanly and headed for the door.

"Tell Jenkins to bring my phaeton round in an hour. I'll be in my study."

He watched Davids leave, and his mood of discontent deepened. He suddenly wished he had never met Lord Bromley, never embroiled himself in the comte's nefarious affairs or left Stanway in the first place. If he had stayed in the country, how different his life would be.

The excitement Roberta felt when she realized she might have found the key to deciphering the list bubbled over. She threw down her pen and stretched her aching back. She had been bent over for an hour or more and now felt very stiff. She pushed back her chair, stood up and danced about the room.

"I've done it!" she sang. "I do believe I have done it!"

And how easy it had been once she had discovered that QFRGJWY actually spelled LAMBERT.

She hugged the knowledge to herself and prayed that Lord Bromley's return was imminent.

Her good humor was still with her when she joined Mrs. Ashley for dinner, greeting her companion with more animation than she had shown in a long while.

"My, my," Mrs. Ashley remarked between mouthfuls of her lobster-stuffed sole. "You are in high spirits tonight."

"Indeed I am, Ashley," she responded gaily.

"I can't imagine what has occurred to make you feel that way. As far as I am aware, you haven't been anywhere or seen anyone. It must be the change in the weather."

Mrs. Ashley studied Roberta skeptically until her attention was claimed by the butler and the tantalizing tray he held. She nodded her acceptance of the varied array of food, and only when her plate was filled did she turn her attention back to the younger woman.

"Perkins informs me we can expect to see Lord Bromley on the morrow," she remarked.

"Tomorrow?" Roberta exclaimed, quickly declining everything the butler offered, except the smallest slice of veal. "What time?"

"Midmorning, I think. I expect you will be pleased to see him."

"Very much so," Roberta remarked. "Do you think he will be pleasantly surprised by the improvement in my health?"

"He will, indeed, although what he will have to say when he hears of our involvement with the comte is another matter entirely. I forgot whether I told you what Sally Jersey had to say of him."

"She knows the comte?"

"Quite intimately, I would say. I asked her about him when she visited with us yesterday. She is very taken by his charm and thinks him a delightful addition to her circle of friends."

"He certainly knows how to charm the elderly," Roberta observed cynically. "Although, even if I had met him under different circumstances, I doubt I would have been taken in. Did Sally Jersey know anything of the affair Sir Nicholas was conducting with the comte's sister?"

"She didn't make mention of it, so I don't think she does. You know how she likes to suppose she's up on every *on-dit* in town. Anyway, I'm just thankful I'm not an intimate member of her circle and that I don't have to acknowledge him."

"You may, dear Ashley, you may. He has promised to pay us a social call in the near future."

"Then I can only pray we are out."

Mrs. Ashley's worst fears were realized the next morning. The butler, without fanfare, announced the comte was downstairs waiting to be received.

"You didn't tell him we were in?" she asked in great agitation.

"No, Mrs. Ashley, but as the hour is still early, I think he assumes you can't have stepped out."

"Oh, dear! Would it be terribly rude of us to deny him, Roberta?"

"Unforgivable," Roberta replied firmly. "We have to face him sometime, Ashley. However, if you really feel unequal to the task, I will receive him alone."

"Never!" Mrs. Ashley retorted with unaccustomed spirit. She stood up quickly and nervously smoothed the creases from her taffeta gown. "For your sake, I will brave this meeting, and I can only hope he realizes that good form dictates it shouldn't last more than twenty minutes."

Roberta turned to the butler. "We will receive him in ten minutes." The servant bowed and withdrew. Roberta pushed the lace curtain back slightly and looked out across the square, where she noticed a man standing beneath the oak tree. She frowned and let the curtain fall back into place. Had he not been there yesterday? And the day before? Could it be that Sir Nicholas had engaged someone to watch the house? She shook her head in bewilderment and then chided herself for being too fanciful. Still, she would mention it to her uncle.

At that moment the comte entered. He paused dramatically on the threshold and, ignoring Mrs. Ashley, smiled at Roberta and strode across the room.

"Mademoiselle Rushforth. I hope you forgive the earliness of my visit. I was afraid you wouldn't be in if I called later in the day."

Roberta inclined her head and forced herself to smile. "We seldom brave the brisk winds before noon," she said, "so we are grateful for any company that will break the tedium of the morning."

His eyes hardened at her veiled snub. "I came to pay my respects to you and your father. How is he?"

"As well as can be expected for a man of his advanced years," she replied, a slight tremor breaking her voice. "He has retired to the country for a while."

"I am sorry to hear that. Perhaps you should have taken more time—broken your trip and spent more than one night at the inns along the way."

Roberta laughed and strove to hide the concern she felt at his obvious probing. "I'm afraid I was responsible for our mad dash and Papa's subsequent exhaustion," she responded. "I gave little thought to my traveling companions' comfort. Is that not correct, Ashley?"

Mrs. Ashley nodded, and Roberta could tell from the way her companion was gripping the arms of her chair that she, too, felt apprehensive. "There was only one thought in her mind, and that was to see an English spring," Mrs. Ashley said. "Although, to my mind, a spring in any country is very pleasant. On the whole, I would have to say it is my favorite season. Do you have any preference, Monsieur le Comte?"

Her voice was slightly higher than normal, but the comte didn't seem to notice. "It would have to be the summer. The warmth of the sun rejuvenates me and prepares me to face another winter."

"And my favorite is autumn," Roberta said, thankful to Mrs. Ashley for turning the conversation so adroitly. "I love the colors the leaves take on. And the crisp air is so pleasant. I do concede, however, it is quite the saddest season, for when the trees lose their leaves, they seem so vulnerable in their nakedness."

The comte smiled at this and then said more softly, "I would like it very much if you would agree to come for a ride with me. I'm considering purchasing Sir Gerald Lynch's roans and would be interested in hearing your opinion of them."

"My opinion? I hardly think I'm qualified to pass judgment on anyone's horseflesh. I haven't ridden, these past two years."

"But I'm told you are very knowledgeable. Lady Jersey makes that claim."

A sudden fear gripped Roberta. If he had talked about her to Sally Jersey, perhaps he had also learned that she had no father. But his next question, asking if her father had taught her to ride, eased her mind slightly. Surely he wouldn't make reference to her fictitious parent if he knew she didn't have one!

"He abhors all exercise," she replied, shaking her head. "My uncle, Lord Bromley, is responsible for my expertise in the saddle. He used to be quite an equestrian in his youth. But as for your request, I shall keep next Monday morning for you. Although, I beg you, please don't expect me to make any comment on the roans."

"Until then I shall wait with ill-concealed impatience." He took her hand and raised it to his lips. "Good day, mademoiselle." He gave Mrs. Ashley a brief bow as Roberta tugged at the bell-rope, and minutes later she watched him from the window as he left the house. The man under the oak tree was still there.

"You will have developed a cold by Monday, or even be stricken by the plague. Anything, Roberta, but you *will not* go for a ride with that—that person," Mrs. Ashley choked.

"It will undoubtedly be the plague," Roberta said with a laugh.

"You—you don't think he suspects anything, do you?" Mrs. Ashley asked anxiously.

"No . . . no," Roberta said slowly. "Not that it will do him much good if he does uncover the truth. We're on English soil now, and there's nothing he can do to harm us." She spoke with more conviction than she felt. In reality, she was worried. The comte was as much an enigma as Sir Nicholas, and she didn't trust either of them.

chapter 10

THE SENSE OF relief Roberta experienced at seeing her uncle was acute, and just after the initial greetings, she asked for a private word with him.

"My dear Roberta, when you adopt that tone with me, I know you have something of the utmost urgency to discuss," he said, his bushy white eyebrows drawn into a playful frown. "I daren't even begin to think what sort of scrape you have embroiled yourself in in so short a time. Why, you have been in England for only a week."

Roberta linked arms with him and pulled him into step with her, ignoring Perkins's plea for a word with his master. "Please come to my sitting room, where we can spend a few minutes undisturbed," she said.

Lord Bromley cast a despairing look at the sheaf of papers Perkins was holding, but allowed himself to be propelled out of the room. "It must be something serious, my gal," he said, patting her hand lightly, "for I've never before known you to be so secretive."

Roberta sighed unhappily. "It's a long story, Uncle, and you're the only person I trust enough to tell."

They had reached Roberta's private rooms by this time, and she quickly closed the door, locking it to insure their privacy. Lord Bromley lowered his large frame into the overstuffed chaise with difficulty.

"First, I want to show you something." Roberta moved over to her desk and pulled out a bundle of papers tied in red ribbon. She riffled through them quickly before joining her uncle on the chaise. "I want you to look at these," she said, handing him the bundle.

Lord Bromley undid the bow and stared uncomprehendingly at the top sheet. "Perhaps you had better explain," he said. "This makes no sense to me whatsoever."

"That, believe it or not, is a list of prominent Englishmen, all engaged in politics and all of whom I know to be friends of yours. At least, some of them are. Three on the list are now deceased."

"Explain yourself, Roberta," Lord Bromley demanded in a low voice as he scanned the remaining papers.

"First let me tell you how the list came into my possession," Roberta said. Without further hesitation, she launched into the circumstances surrounding her meeting Sir Nicholas and all the events that had occurred since.

"Dear Lord!" Lord Bromley exclaimed somberly. "I know I must believe it, but even so, I find it difficult. Are you sure of your facts, Roberta?"

"I only know that I took a certain paper from Sir Nicholas's cabin, of which this is a copy, and yesterday managed to decipher it."

"I'm trying to follow you, but I confess bewilderment. How do you equate this gibberish," he inquired patiently, holding the top sheet aloft, "with your interpretation?"

"It was something Stephen Davenport said when he called on me yesterday. He told me the comte was seeking introductions to various politicians, and Mr. Lambert was one of the names he mentioned. Now, if you notice, on the paper I took from Sir Nicholas, there is only one set of letters that has seven digits. See, this one here. QFRGJWY." Lord Bromley nodded. "I merely worked on the presumption that it stood for Lambert."

"And so from that you were able to deduce everyone else's name? It makes no sense, Roberta, no sense at all."

"But it does, Uncle. I don't pretend to know what it all means, but I'm certain I'm correct in my findings. The code is really the simplest. The comte has merely added five letters to the original, in order to confuse a casual observer. And, as simple as it might be, it is quite effective, because, unless you have a specific name to work with, it is meaningless."

Lord Bromley looked at her speculatively for a moment.

"A very clever piece of work, Roberta. I am forced to agree with your findings."

"That's why I wanted to see you so urgently. You see, I—I suspect that Sir Nicholas is a spy. And, what is more, I think he has someone watching this house."

This last piece of information drew a mild oath from Lord Bromley, and Roberta smiled triumphantly.

"I knew you wouldn't like hearing that," she murmured, "especially since, in your capacity of Under Secretary, you receive some very strange visitors. It would do you a great deal of harm, wouldn't it, if some of your callers were stopped and questioned after they left this house?"

"Dammit, Roberta, that's none of your business!"

"I know, Uncle, and I promise I won't mention it again. What worries me now is the fact that Sir Nicholas had several more papers with him. They could either be additional names or, possibly, instructions about gathering information the French government wants." She paused expectantly, waiting for some comment. But Lord Bromley, deep in thought, remained silent. "Is my reasoning so farfetched, Uncle?"

He shook his head slowly, a troubled expression on his face. "You've simply no idea what you've embroiled yourself in, Roberta. I need time to assimilate all the facts you have presented me with."

"But what about Sir Nicholas?" Roberta demanded. "Is he to be allowed to wander about London at will?"

Lord Bromley was saved from having to answer by a knock on the door. Roberta stepped over to it, unlocked it, and with an impatient gesture, threw it open. Perkins stood outside, an envelope clutched in his hand.

"I'm sorry to disturb you, Miss Roberta," he said, "but an urgent dispatch has arrived for Lord Bromley."

"Oh, very well! Although I don't think it can be any more important than the discussion I'm trying to have with my uncle."

"What is it, Perkins?" Lord Bromley called out. "Come on in, for goodness' sake. I can't abide talking to people I can't see."

"This has just come, my lord," Perkins said as he entered. "The messenger seemed a trifle concerned when I told him you were engaged, so, under the circumstances, I thought I had better seek you out at once."

"Who was it?" Lord Bromley asked brusquely as he took the envelope from his secretary and extracted the enclosed letter. "The usual one?"

"Eh—eh! No, my lord," he returned softly, looking at Roberta with some concern. "It was Jenkins."

"Then tell him not to come here again. My niece seems to think that we are being watched. Have you noticed anything untoward?"

"There certainly has been an increase of activity in the square since Miss Roberta's return, my lord, but I can't say that I have seen obvious signs of anyone lingering about the house without reason."

"We'll use my club as a meeting place for the time being," Lord Bromley said as he returned the letter and Roberta's papers to the envelope. "Inform the obvious people immediately, Perkins." He rose from the chaise and crossed to the window. "I have to go out now, but I will see you in my study later on this afternoon."

"Very good, my lord," Perkins answered, and departed quickly.

"As for you, my gal," Lord Bromley continued, "I want you to try and forget all this nonsense of lists and names. We can continue our discussion when I return." As he spoke, he looked out of the window, and saw the man Roberta had described. "It certainly is an odd place to choose to stand all day with nothing to do," he murmured. "The Strand would be far more interesting, I would have thought."

"Then you don't think he is there watching us?" Roberta asked.

"I don't know what to think as yet, but as I said, if he's not watching us, what *is* he doing? Now, don't do anything foolish in my absence. I'll return as quickly as possible."

"But I haven't finished yet, Uncle," Roberta protested unhappily. "Something else has happened that could cause even greater complication."

"It will have to wait." He shook his head one last time before dropping the curtain. "I wonder what he hopes to learn by having the house watched?" On that cryptic note, he left, leaving Roberta feeling thoroughly frustrated.

She tried to occupy herself by working on a sampler, but made so many mistakes that she gave up in disgust. Finally, she put on her cloak, exchanged her cap for a bonnet and went for a short stroll with Polly, her new lady's maid, following a few paces behind.

She deliberately went out of her way to gain access to the gardens, in order to pass the man by the oak tree. She stared at him openly, uncaring that she might arouse his suspicions. Before he bent over to sharpen some knives that lay at his feet, she noticed he had a small scar above his right eye. His complexion was ruddy, as though he had spent a lot of time outdoors, and his sharp features reminded her of a weasel.

"Is that your trade?" she asked loudly.

He nodded. "It's not a crime as I knows of," he muttered in surly tones. "I can practice me craft anywheres I choose, can't I?"

"All week in the same spot!" she exclaimed. "Unless, of course, every household knife in the square is blunt. However, I think you would be very foolish to select the same position tomorrow, for I have become a trifle bored by your constant presence." She moved away, and consequently failed to see the sly look he cast her way.

"Miss Rushforth? Good morning."

She turned quickly and saw Sir Nicholas in his phaeton, reining in an exquisite pair of high-stepping horses. His man—whom Sir Nicholas called Jenkins, Roberta noted with interest—was perched behind him.

"Would you mind if I joined you for a short walk?"

She was about to refuse when a sudden, darting movement from the knife sharpener, as though he were trying to hide, made her change her mind.

She nodded. "Please do," she said hastily when she realized that Sir Nicholas was having difficulty restraining the horses. "I'm beginning to find my own company rather tedious."

Sir Nicholas jumped down and handed the reins to Jenkins, instructing his servant to walk the animals.

"Tell me, Miss Rushforth," he said as he took Roberta's arm, "do you normally walk along public thoroughfares with your maid trailing so far behind? When I first saw you, I thought you were unchaperoned."

There was a note of disapproval in his voice, and Roberta stiffened in anger. "I hardly think that is any of your concern, Sir Nicholas. I told you once before that I'm not a girl just out of the schoolroom. As it happens, I was merely going to the gardens."

"Then I'm glad I happened by before you reached the gate, else I would have missed you," Sir Nicholas responded, deliberately ignoring her anger.

"Were you seeking my company, then?" she inquired with false sweetness.

"I am supposed to be dangling after you," he replied rather nonchalantly.

"There is no need to continue with the sham any longer. My uncle has returned, and he can protect me now from the comte and any other dangers that present themselves."

"I hope you won't give me the cold shoulder yet," he returned earnestly. "I don't think my standing in Society is such that I can afford an abrupt dismissal from you."

"You put too much store on my influence, Sir Nicholas. If you care so much about approval, you should follow the comte's lead and ingratiate yourself with Sally Jersey. Once you have gained her approval, you know, everyone will accept you without question."

"Dear Sally. 'Tis her recognition I fear more than anyone's. She's such a dratted bore."

"Sir Nicholas!" Roberta exclaimed in scandalized tones. "You must never be that careless with your remarks. Why, if I were to repeat what you just said, you would be ostracized immediately."

"In a more civilised society than ours, it would have needed at least six thousand votes before such a dreadful catastrophe could have overtaken me," he observed with a grin.

"Aha! The Athenians and their democracy," Roberta replied, determined to prove that she knew her Greek history. "Well, equate, if you can, a Greek marketplace with Almack's. Someone arbitrarily decides that a certain person is dangerous and unwholesome. In Greece, the Athenians would merely write the name of the undesirable on an ostrakon. If six thousand ostrakons were cast, the unfortunate victim was banished for six years. In England, it only needs one person—namely, Sally Jersey—to say that Mr. So-

and-so is despicable, and that poor victim is banished for an equal length of time from Society. So please, Sir Nicholas, take my advice and don't utter such banalities unless you wish to be ostracized."

"Miss Rushforth, you are an extremely refreshing change. There is no other woman of my acquaintance who would know about ostrakons. Are you as fascinated as I am by the development of the English language?"

"Now, that, Sir Nicholas, is a leading question. If I were to agree with you, you would immediately dub me a blue-stocking."

"But surely you wouldn't be averse to being compared to Elizabeth Montagu? She, after all, was the forerunner of what we now call 'women of intellectual persuasions.'"

"Of course not. She was a remarkably courageous woman, Sir Nicholas. The fact that she wore blue stockings as a symbol of her beliefs, and allowed herself to be ridiculed by Admiral Buscawen, is not something I'm likely to forget. Unfortunately, the term has taken on a different connotation in present-day Society, and no woman wishes to be considered affectedly studious."

"I take your point, but your very knowledge of ostrakons and Admiral Buscawen is an indication of your interest in the development of our language."

"Then I shall take care in the future to address myself only to such topics as the weather and the latest fashions."

"I cannot believe you really mean that," Sir Nicholas said, his eyes twinkling in amusement. "If I am not mistaken, you enjoy being regarded as an original, and that is a title you would lose if you only addressed yourself to such commonplace topics."

"Tell me, Sir Nicholas," Roberta said abruptly, "did you ever know a Mr. Lambert?" She was pleased to note his frown at the unexpectedness of her question. "Or Geoffrey Laurie?"

"I don't understand your questions, Miss Rushforth" he responded uneasily. "Why should I know these people?"

"I'm curious, Sir Nicholas, merely curious." She took a deep breath. "You see, I copied that piece of paper I took from your cabin, and they were but two of the names on the list."

"I find that very interesting," he said slowly, as though weighing his words carefully. "But, as far as I can recall, the letters on that paper were random ones—nonsense, you might say."

"You might say what you please, Sir Nicholas. I *know* it was a code."

"A remarkably astute deduction, if I may say so. And now that you are in possession of this information, what do you propose to do with it?"

Roberta looked at him quizzically. She had hoped to disconcert him with her revelations, but he looked remarkably self-possessed.

"I haven't quite decided," she said finally. "However, I think the comte will be interested."

"For an intelligent woman, Miss Rushforth, you are displaying a great deal of ignorance. With the facts that you have at your disposal, I'm surprised you haven't deduced the truth."

"Truth, Sir Nicholas! Since when has the truth bothered you?" she retorted. She was annoyed by his refusal to be drawn. "You burst into my life, and I thought you were dead. When it became apparent that you weren't, you foisted yourself upon Mrs. Ashley and myself in order to make your escape from France. Add to that the occasions I have had to endure improper advances from yourself and the comte, to bear the constant snooping of your watchdog posing as a knife sharpener. What time have I had to deduce anything?"

"My watchdog, Miss Rushforth? I'm afraid I don't understand. To what are you referring?"

"Don't toy with me, Sir Nicholas. I'm aware of the man you have posted outside my uncle's house. Were you surprised to learn that Stephen Davenport visited me and that I received him personally? Would you like to know what transpired at that meeting?" She broke off in some confusion as she became aware of Sir Nicholas's bemused glance. It was perfectly obvious he had no idea what she was talking about. "I suppose you are going to deny any knowledge of such a man?"

Sir Nicholas nodded. "However, you are right about one thing, Miss Rushforth. I would dearly love to know what you discussed with Stephen Davenport."

"You—you—Oh! You're insufferable!" Roberta snapped. "Take me home, please," she said, brushing her brow wearily. "You have exhausted my patience, and I can see no point in continuing this conversation."

Sir Nicholas gripped her arm tightly. "Will you promise me one thing, Miss Rushforth?" he asked softly, his voice filled with concern.

Roberta shivered at his touch. She could feel his warm breath on her cheek, and for a moment she thought he was going to kiss her. His nearness was suffocating, yet she was incapable of moving away. She turned to face him, her eyes open wide, and the peak of her bonnet brushed his nose. The tension between them increased.

"Don't look at me like that, Miss Rushforth," he said hoarsely, "else I might lose my grip on my self-control."

She parted her lips and shook her head in confusion. By rights, she should be angry with him, but instead she wanted nothing more than to feel his lips on hers. She lifted her head slightly, still mesmerized. In that instant, she experienced a gamut of emotions that left her breathless. Her fingers, with a seeming will of their own, reached out to touch his cheek. Dimly she heard him exhale sharply, and then he jerked his face away. It was white with strain. Her hand fell, and she finally emerged from her hypnotic state, shaken and abashed.

"Forgive me, Sir Nicholas," she said in a strained voice. "I can't think what came over me. You wanted to extract a promise from me?"

He stared blankly at her for a moment and then shook his head. "It's of no importance," he replied, obviously as shaken as herself by what had just occurred. "I'll take you home now."

He turned and started to retrace his steps to Grosvenor Square. Roberta followed him meekly.

chapter 11

"I'M ASHAMED TO SAY, Uncle, that I allowed my tongue to run away with me," Roberta was saying an hour later to Lord Bromley. They were ensconced in the blue room, and Roberta was nervously pacing the floor. "I questioned Sir Nicholas about the names on that list."

"You did *what*, Roberta?" Lord Bromley expostulated. "Have you taken leave of all your senses?"

"I was suddenly seized by this madcap idea that if I confronted him directly, I would surprise the truth out of him."

"Madcap, indeed. What on earth could have gotten into you? You don't normally act so foolishly. Do you realize the danger you have put yourself in? If this Sir Nicholas is as guilty of treason as you would have me believe, he could have you silenced immediately with one thrust of a knife. Did that not occur to you?"

Roberta had never seen her uncle so angry before, and she did her best to appease him. But he refused to listen to her excuses and continued to upbraid her.

"The next thing you'll be telling me is that you have confided all this nonsense to the comte," he said sarcastically. "And, no doubt, you will say that you were seized with another madcap scheme."

Roberta started guiltily at this, for she had suggested that very possibility to Sir Nicholas. "I wouldn't be so stupid, Uncle. After all I've done to save the neck of that—that ungrateful—nay, hateful—man, I'm not likely to throw him back to his tormentor."

"That is not what I heard," Lord Bromley said carelessly, and then frowned at his slip.

"What exactly have you heard, Uncle?" she demanded, suddenly intrigued. "I have only made mention to one person of the possibility that I might confide in the comte, and that was no more than two hours ago."

"Drat you, my gal. Sometimes you are too clever for your own good."

"Tell me about Sir Nicholas, Uncle," she begged, her interest now fully roused. "If you wish to silence my tongue, you must explain why Sir Nicholas sought you out today."

"I don't have to explain anything to you, Roberta. However, in the interest of your own self-preservation, I will break with my usual silence and tell you a few pertinent facts."

Roberta sat down and folded her hands in her lap. She knew better than to break her uncle's concentration with any interruption.

"Perkins tells me you had a visitor this morning."

"The comte," Roberta confirmed. "He came to inquire after Papa's health, and to ask me to go for a ride with him on Monday."

A look of concern lit Lord Bromley's deep-set eyes. "You won't go, of course," he said as he sat down next to her. "And that is an order." He stared at the flames dancing in the fireplace, and then suddenly turned to face her. "Look at me, Roberta." She complied quickly. "You know that in my capacity as Under Secretary, a lot of my work is of a secret nature?" Roberta nodded. "And that normally I do not speak of it to anyone outside government circles?" Again Roberta nodded. "What I am about to impart to you, Roberta, is so confidential, so delicate, that if one word leaks out, a whole year's work will be wasted, and countless people will suffer. Do I have your word that you will remain silent, and do your best to forget what I am about to tell you?"

"Yes, Uncle," Roberta responded quietly. The deadly seriousness with which her uncle addressed her had filled her with alarm. "No provocation, no matter how great, will force me to repeat anything you say."

"That list of names you deciphered—I think it is a list

of men who are being blackmailed by the comte."

"Good heavens!" she exclaimed. "Whatever for?"

"Secrets, Roberta," he responded heavily. "Military and political. All of them vital to this nation's security. For the past twelve months, I have been trying to discover what hold he has had on my friends that would force them to talk of such delicate matters. Because by nature, none of these is a traitor. Whatever this hold is, has, unfortunately, eluded me thus far. I must find out, though, and quickly. I also must discover exactly what information he has extracted from them. However, thanks to Sir Nicholas, we now know the names of the men he has either used or is planning to use."

"Sir Nicholas?" Roberta breathed shakily. "You mean Sir Nicholas is working for you?" The relief she felt at this disclosure caused her to laugh. "I had convinced myself he was working for the French. How could I have been so blind?"

"He's a clever young man, good—nay, excellent—at his work. You assumed what you did because that is what he wanted you to think. He would have preferred that you remain in ignorance of his background, but I have deemed it too perilous to our cause. There is no one more dangerous than the person who only knows half the truth."

Roberta bowed her head sheepishly. "I feel so ashamed of myself," she murmured.

"There, there, my gal. Now that you know the truth, you will be more discreet."

"How did Sir Nicholas manage to acquire the papers?"

"He penetrated the comte's household. Goodness knows, it wasn't easy, and without Henri and Marie, he never would have succeeded."

"I am beginning to see just what harm a few careless words to the comte might have caused," she murmured. "I had no idea, no idea at all. This affair that Sir Nicholas had with the comte's sister, was that part of the plan as well?"

"It was a deliberate ploy. There was no other way he could gain access to the fortress the comte calls his home."

The answer was all she wanted to hear—and she was delighted she had misjudged him! "What a dangerous thing to have to do. Why, his true motives could have been un-covered at any time!"

"Oh, the woman wasn't without certain charms," Lord Bromley said lightly. "He knew the risk he was taking, but he is a man who puts the honor of his country before his own safety. Unfortunately, for my sake, there aren't many like him."

"I hope he didn't lose his heart to this *femme fatale*," she responded. "Marie said she is a beautiful woman."

"What, and risk jeopardizing everything? No, my dear, Sir Nicholas is not a man to lose his heart to any woman."

"It is certainly the impression he gives," she said. "He is a self-contained person, quite obviously wedded to his work." The truth of her words made her feel strangely de-flated, and she was forced to wonder why he had acted so oddly during their walk.

"As for you, Roberta," Lord Bromley continued gruffly, "I'm afraid I'm going to have to spoil your return to En-gland. I have made arrangements to send you to the country for the duration of the comte's visit here. I can't think of any other way of giving you adequate protection."

"No, Uncle!" she cried. "It's unfair of you to expect me to do such a thing. My absence is bound to cause all sorts of wild speculation about my health."

Lord Bromley shook his head. "My mind is made up, Roberta."

"Is Sir Nicholas behind all this?" she asked shrewdly. "Is he the one who wants me out of the way?"

"It was his suggestion, but a sound one nonetheless."

"And how do you propose to seek the solution to the greatest dilemma facing you now?" she demanded with a cunning born of desperation. "Namely, what information does the comte have that enables him to blackmail your colleagues?"

"I refuse to discuss any further aspects of my work with you, Roberta. You already know far too much for your own good."

"You refuse, Uncle, because you have no ready answers. Well, I have a plan, and it's the only one, in my estimation, that has a chance of succeeding quickly."

"And it undoubtedly calls for your presence in London," Lord Bromley said dryly.

"How astute of you." Roberta laughed. "I propose that I actively encourage the comte's pursuit of me. At the risk of sounding immodest, I—I know he is not indifferent to my charms. You know as well as anyone that a man can be extraordinarily indiscreet in the presence of a lady, especially a lady he is trying to woo. Why should the comte be any different? A little flattery from me, a few naive questions about his work—oh! There are countless ways a woman could uncover the necessary information where no man ever could."

"You are a scheming little minx, my dear," Lord Bromley said with a laugh.

A pained expression crossed her face. "Not scheming, Uncle," she said in injured tones. "Just logical."

"You place me in a very difficult position. There is a certain urgency involved in this matter which makes it impossible for me to refuse your request. I need to know what the comte is using to blackmail my colleagues, before another of them is murdered or kills himself." His voice was heavy with regret, and he shook his head sadly. "But to involve someone I look upon as my own daughter, why, it's abhorrent to me."

"I won't do anything foolhardy," Roberta assured him quickly. "And I will certainly do everything in my power to bring about that fiend's downfall. Poor Mr. Lambert, poor Willie. The comte has a lot to account for, hasn't he?"

Lord Bromley nodded. "There are two conditions I must place upon you before I give my final consent to this—this plan of yours," he said as he stood up. "First, you will not leave this house unless you have either Mrs. Ashley, Williams or Polly with you. I know I have turned a blind eye in the past when you have sallied out unchaperoned," he added as Roberta pulled a wry face. "However, it is unseemly behavior, and I do not approve of it at all.

"Second," he continued, "you will have to bear with Sir Nicholas's attentions at all social functions you attend. He can pretend that he is smitten by your charm. He has all the right credentials to gain entry to the same affairs as you, and he can be on hand to protect you from the comte, should it become necessary."

"If you insist, Uncle," she said, "but I don't think Sir Nicholas will agree so readily to such a scheme."

"He will," Lord Bromley averred. "He is as anxious as I to put an end to the comte's game."

"And, like you, dear Uncle, he will use anyone he can to gain this victory?"

The slight touch of bitterness that tinged her voice caused Lord Bromley to look at her sharply, but she smiled up at him sweetly, and he relaxed again. "Yes," he said.

"We could begin this charade tomorrow," she said, joining her uncle by the fireplace. "Lady Winthrop is holding a masked fancy-dress ball."

"Did the comte say he would be present?"

"No, but I'm sure if he hears I intend to go, he will make the necessary arrangements to be there."

"And how do you propose he find out?"

"Lady Jersey has invited me to tea this afternoon," she returned nonchalantly. "Knowing her penchant for gossip, if I tell her I shall be attending, the whole of London will know by nightfall."

"You seem very confident of yourself, my dear."

"I am," Roberta said, recalling with a shudder the intimate way the comte had caressed her hand that morning. "The comte will undoubtedly seize the opportunity that such an informal gathering presents to accost me. The only thing is, will Sir Nicholas agree to attend as well?"

"You can ask him yourself, my dear," Lord Bromley responded, a sudden twinkle in his eyes. "He is due here any minute now."

As if on cue, the butler entered and coughed discreetly. "Your late-afternoon appointment has arrived, my lord," he said. "Shall I have him wait?"

"No, no. Ask him to join us."

Roberta moved to a small writing desk set in an alcove and leaned against it for support. Her legs felt weak at the thought of seeing Sir Nicholas again so soon. She had only just positioned herself when the door swung open once more, and a portly, bowlegged, immaculately dressed old man teetered into the room on bright red shoes with overly high heels.

She glanced at him sharply and then looked to her uncle for an introduction. Her uncle, however, was smiling warmly at the newcomer and advancing toward him, a hand outstretched in greeting. Only then did she realize that she was looking at Sir Nicholas.

"A fine disguise, my boy," Lord Bromley commented heartily. "Our little friend outside will have a difficult time identifying you for the comte."

Sir Nicholas laughed, a deep, resonant sound that Roberta easily recognized. "I thought it a necessary precaution, John, but it's damned uncomfortable and deuced hot. Davids insisted on all this padding, though why I ever let him persuade me to don these dreadful creepers and galligaskins is beyond my comprehension. I swear I would rather die a young man than to have to face the prospect of wearing such cumbersome things in my dotage."

"Such a prospect seems unlikely, Sir Nicholas, given your line of work," Roberta observed mildly. Her presence in the room obviously caught him unawares, for he wheeled around in surprise.

"Miss Rushforth!" he exclaimed, making as elegant a leg as he could manage. "I had no idea you were here. Please forgive my unwitting rudeness."

His easy manner helped her overcome the embarrassment she felt at seeing him again, and she was thankful he made no reference to their earlier meeting.

"I asked her to stay a moment," Lord Bromley interjected, "while I explain to you the slight modification of the plan we discussed over luncheon."

Sir Nicholas was frowning his disapproval by the time Lord Bromley had finished his explanation.

"I like it no more than you, Nicholas," Lord Bromley said. "But we are pressed for time, and this scheme of Roberta's offers the most expedient way out of our dilemma. She's not lacking for common sense, and I know we can rely on her discretion."

"'Tis not that that bothers me," Sir Nicholas replied slowly, ignoring Roberta's presence, much to her annoyance. "I can't like the fact that she will deliberately set out to win the comte's affections. He doesn't live by the same code of honor as you or I. He takes what he wants, when he wants, and discards it when he's had his fill. If he really is an enamored of her as he would have her believe, then he will act ruthlessly until he has achieved his end."

"If you are alluding to his possessing me, Sir Nicholas," Roberta interposed, "let me allay your fears. I shall carry with me at all times the small pistol my uncle gave me. I will not hesitate to use it if the occasion arises."

Sir Nicholas raised his eyebrows at this piece of bravado and looked to Lord Bromley for confirmation.

"Aye, it's the truth; she is a remarkable shot. I taught her myself."

"I hope your disapproval of my plan doesn't mean that you will be reluctant to offer me your protection," Roberta said in a deliberate attempt to goad Sir Nicholas. She found his high-handed manner of dispassionately discussing her extremely irksome. But he didn't rise to her bait, and to her further annoyance, he shook his head and continued his conversation with Lord Bromley.

"You may rest assured, John, that I will do everything in my power to prevent Miss Rushforth having to resort to such an act."

"Quite so, quite so," Lord Bromley said hastily.

"At least you won't have to rig yourself out in such a ridiculous garb each time you want to see my uncle in private," Roberta said, stubbornly refusing to be excluded.

"I thank you for your consideration, Miss Rushforth," he murmured. "That, indeed, will be a welcome relief."

She nodded briefly and took her leave, satisfied that she had made her point. "If I am to visit Lady Jersey, I had best go now. You see, Sir Nicholas, I thought to go to the masked ball Lady Winthrop is holding tomorrow night," she said airily as she crossed to the door. "That is, if I can persuade you to attend as well."

"Is the comte to be there?" he asked.

"I'm sure he will be, once he hears of my intentions from Lady Jersey."

Sir Nicholas looked annoyed but gave his reluctant agreement. "Although, in the future, Miss Rushforth, I would appreciate it if you would give me advance warning of the affairs you wish to attend, for, as is the case tomorrow, I may already have a prior engagement."

"I have no desire to interfere with your personal life," Roberta responded coldly. "There is no need for us to go to this masked romp."

"I have agreed to escort you, Miss Rushforth," Sir Nicholas replied with growing irritation. "I will present myself here at ten tomorrow night."

Roberta curtsied and departed without another word. She felt much better now that she had finally managed to put him on the defensive. She would prove to him once and for all that she wasn't a woman who accepted such treatment without fighting back.

Her smile broadened into a grin. "I do believe I'm going to enjoy myself enormously," she murmured with a laugh. "And it will be entirely at your expense, Sir Nicholas."

The small tea party to which Lady Jersey had invited Roberta and Mrs. Ashley was well underway by the time they arrived.

"I knew we would be the last to get here," Mrs. Ashley said nervously as the butler announced them. "Perhaps it would have been better had we not come at all."

There was no time for Roberta to reassure her companion, because Lady Jersey swooped down on them. "My dear Roberta, Mrs. Ashley," she said, her face wreathed in smiles. "How perfectly wonderful that you could come. I had almost despaired of seeing you."

"Then you forgive our tardiness?" Roberta said, patiently suffering Lady Jersey's embrace. "I'm afraid I'm at fault. My uncle has just returned to London, and I spent more time than I should have, talking to him."

"And how is dear Lord Bromley? No, don't tell me. I'm certain he's as well as he ever has been. Such a lovely man, and such a puzzlement to me that he has never married. Now, let me see, who can I introduce you to?"

Roberta glanced around and smiled at several people she recognized. "I think I know everyone," she murmured. "If you don't mind, I'll go and say hello to Lady Jenny." She moved away, leaving Mrs. Ashley to the mercy of their hostess.

Roberta kept a watchful eye on Lady Jersey all during tea. When it appeared that her hostess had tired of flitting between her guests, she approached her tentatively.

"Excuse me, Lady Jersey," she said. "I was wondering if you could give me some advice."

"Advice? Why, yes, my dear. That, as the whole of London knows, is the one thing I dispense with pleasure."

Roberta smiled. "It's about tomorrow night. I don't quite know what to wear. You see, having been out of the country for so long, I'm no longer familiar with what's considered proper attire."

"Ah," Lady Jersey replied, "but everyone I know is undecided what they should wear. As you have already enjoyed several Seasons, I think it would be quite appropriate if you wore something striking—a dress that will catch everyone's attention. You should never be frightened of revealing your charms. I never was, and it didn't harm my standing in society."

"I shall let myself be guided by you, then, Lady Jersey, and go as a French courtesan. I bought a gown in France that would do very nicely."

"Ah! the French. They certainly lead us in fashion, don't they?" She eyed Roberta speculatively and then chuckled. "And Frenchmen are masters in the art of dalliance. They're so romantic, don't you think?"

"I . . . eh . . . my experience is limited," Roberta replied. "The comte is the only Frenchman I know."

"And it was he I was referring to. He's so delightfully wicked. He speaks highly of you, Roberta, and will be pleased to know that you will be at Lady Winthrop's. You should feel encouraged that you have two of London's most eligible gentlemen dangling after you."

"I think you exaggerate matters, Lady Jersey!" Roberta exclaimed with becoming modesty.

"But, my dear, everyone is talking about the way Sir Nicholas has singled you out. Why, Lady Ramsden was saying just before you arrived, that she believed his intentions must be serious. Mind you, her reason for suggesting such a thing is because she failed to persuade him to take an interest in that poor daughter of hers last year."

"Cynthia?"

Lady Jersey nodded. "Although I do hasten to add that there is a vast difference between you and Cynthia. Why, the girl has managed to inherit the worst traits of both her parents. She's inclined to plumpness, she stammers and she makes no pretense of the fact that she prefers to read rather than to dance. I sometimes feel I am being remiss in my duty by not advising Lady Ramsden she is wasting her time in pushing Cynthia, especially as she has three other daughters to settle."

"I have always found Cynthia to be a most engaging young lady," Roberta demurred. "She accepts her shortcomings with grace, and does her best to please her mama. It is perhaps unfortunate, don't you think, that some females are more blessed than others in their looks?"

"Looks are everything," Lady Jersey responded firmly. "No man wants to be shackled to a dowdy bluestocking."

"Yet how many men enjoy being shackled to an empty mind when their lady's bloom has faded?"

"No matter what your age, Roberta, you are still an innocent. Men can always find ways of enjoying themselves outside the home."

Before Roberta could reply, somebody claimed Lady Jersey's attention, and she breathed a sigh of relief, for she found Lady Jersey's manner altogether too overbearing.

"In the unlikely event that I ever marry," she murmured crossly, "I will make it perfectly clear to my spouse that I will not countenance his finding outside distractions."

"You look positively annoyed about something," Mrs. Ashley said as she joined Roberta. "You mustn't let Lady Jersey's tongue overset you."

"Oh dear!" Roberta said guiltily. "I didn't realize my face reflected my thoughts. Perhaps we should go before I disagree with anyone else."

As they made their farewells, Lady Jersey whispered that she would endeavor to present a certain Frenchman to Roberta at the masked ball. The younger woman smiled in satisfaction.

chapter 12

"WHAT DO YOU think, Polly?" Roberta asked as she turned slowly in front of the mirror. "Will anyone recognize me?"

Polly shook her head and looked away in some confusion. Her mistress was behaving in a very strange manner, one she couldn't understand at all. And the dress she was wearing was now almost indecent. Without the lace insert, the bodice revealed an ample portion of bosom.

"I don't 'ardly think so, Miss Roberta," she said at last. "I've never seen you look so . . . I mean, you don't look like a lady at all."

Roberta laughed. "I'm not supposed to, Polly," she explained to the young girl. "I've dressed as I think a French courtesan would, for it is important that I attract a certain gentleman's attention tonight." She smoothed an imaginary crease from the close-fitting skirt, which caused the soft folds of silk chiffon to hug her legs closely. "I hope I have the courage to bear the ogling glances I'm bound to draw."

"Mrs. Ashley will be most upset when she sees you," Polly ventured. "Do you really 'ave to go to such lengths?"

"Dear Polly, you mustn't worry. Sir Nicholas will give me all the protection I need. And Ashley won't see my gown until we have arrived at Lady Winthrop's. I will don my cloak before I leave the bedroom."

The hint of excitement in Roberta's voice was infectious, and Polly nodded secretively. It suddenly occurred to her that her mistress was really trying to attract Sir Nicholas but was using the other gentleman as bait. And with that thought, a tiny flame of hope was rekindled in her own heart. If her mistress succeeded in attaching Sir Nicholas, then perhaps she would not have to forego her own future happiness with Davids, the man she loved.

"Hurry, Polly," Roberta urged as the hall clock chimed. "My cloak and mask. I don't want to be late."

Polly deftly placed the cloak about Roberta's shoulders and stood back to insure that her mistress's dress was well concealed.

Roberta swept gracefully out of the room. Just as she reached the bottom of the sweeping staircase, Mrs. Ashley joined her.

"I declare, I am quite looking forward to this evening," Mrs. Ashley said. "I shall enjoy watching the pageantry of the various costumes. Are you still going to keep me in suspense about yours? I think I should know what you are wearing, in case I lose sight of you in the crush."

"You won't, Ashley. I'll make certain of that."

"I thought I heard your voice, Roberta," Lord Bromley said as he emerged from his study. "You'd best be off before you miss all the festivities. I hear there is to be a firework display of uncommon brilliance."

Roberta smiled and kissed his cheek. "Good night, Uncle. I will see you in the morning to tell you all that transpires."

"I won't be here," he said somewhat evasively. "But if anything happens, I'm bound to hear about it."

Roberta frowned and was about to ask where he was going, when the butler announced that the carriage was waiting.

"I do hope the heat won't be overpowering," Mrs. Ashley remarked, blissfully unaware of Roberta's distracted mood. "I almost fainted away at the last of Lady Winthrop's I attended."

"I will insure that you are seated by the windows in the ballroom, Ashley, for, if my memory serves me correctly, they do not create too much of a draught when opened."

They had settled themselves in the carriage by this time, and Roberta turned to wave to her uncle. He lifted his hand in a half-salute and disappeared back inside the house. Roberta stared out of the window, a thoughtful expression on her face. She had the oddest notion that something had happened to do with the comte and that her uncle was deliberately keeping her in the dark about it. Well, if the opportunity arose, she would ask Sir Nicholas.

The rest of the journey was completed in silence. They had just donned their masks when the door of their carriage was flung open by a hired flunkey, who competently helped the two ladies to alight. A red canopy, brilliantly lit by hundreds of candles, covered their short walk into the flower-decked hall. More servants were there to relieve them of their cloaks, and Roberta prepared herself for Mrs. Ashley's criticism of her dress. But her companion's attention had been caught by the hideous garb of an unknown dandy dressed as a court jester.

"Good heavens, Roberta!" she exclaimed. "I declare, my head aches already, just looking at those awful colors."

Roberta laughed and quickly pulled her shawl over her shoulders. Mrs. Ashley turned her attention back to Roberta and nodded approvingly. "You look absolutely charming, my dear," she said. "That is a most becoming dress."

"Why, thank you Ashley," Roberta replied, and with great determination pushed her troubled thoughts away. There would be plenty of time later to find out why her uncle had behaved so evasively.

They joined the throng of people already making their way up the great staircase, and as Lady Winthrop had dispensed with the formality of greeting her guests, Roberta and Mrs. Ashley soon found themselves in the ballroom. A few couples were already dancing.

Their progress as they circled the waxed floor was slow. Several men stopped Roberta and asked for her card, onto which they penciled their initials beside the dance of their choice. She didn't recognize any of them, and worried for a moment that her card would be filled before Sir Nicholas or the comte arrived. But Mrs. Ashley's next words put that fear to rest.

"That must be Sir Nicholas, Roberta. Over there—the man in the red domino."

Roberta looked in the direction of Mrs. Ashley's gaze and nodded. It was not difficult to recognize him. He stood several inches above his nearby companion and had made no effort to powder his hair. His eyes were sweeping the room and rested on Roberta briefly. She raised a hand and waved to attract his attention before continuing on her way.

It would be up to him, she decided, to seek her out. However, she took the precaution of marking off two dances on her card, one of them the supper dance.

She had just finished making Mrs. Ashley comfortable in a chair when Sir Nicholas wandered over. He bowed low over Mrs. Ashley's hand, and Roberta sensed he was deliberately ignoring her.

"Good evening," she murmured in dulcet tones. "Would it be considered forward of me if I presented myself to the red domino? I trust you had no difficulty rearranging your appointment to accommodate this whim of mine for tonight's entertainment?"

A frown, swift but deep, crossed Sir Nicholas's face as he made his bow to Roberta, but there was no time for him to respond, for a friend of Mrs. Ashley's joined them.

"You don't have to concern yourself over me now, Roberta," Mrs. Ashley said indulgently. "It's an age since I last saw Mrs. Swanson, and while you young things enjoy yourselves, we can indulge in a comfortable coze."

Roberta smiled and moved away. Sir Nicholas followed her.

"You will stay in the ballroom until the comte approaches you," he said curtly. "Assuming, of course, that he is here tonight. You must not make the mistake of appearing too eager or willing. He is a man who responds to challenge, not easy conquest."

"I shall bear that in mind, Sir Nicholas," she returned with ill-concealed annoyance.

"Your card, if you please, Miss Rushforth."

"I have already reserved the supper dance for you," Roberta said, but she gave him the card anyway.

He looked at it briefly, put his name beside the last dance as well and then returned it to her. "I hope you won't have tired yourself out before the end of the evening," he said, a heavy scowl creasing his face.

"You really must do better than this if you are to convince the ton that you are one of my suitors," Roberta chided gently. "You don't look as though you are enjoying my company at all."

"Happily, my mask will cover my true feelings tonight," he said sharply.

Sir Nicholas's obvious displeasure suddenly began to

pall. In an effort to appease him, Roberta apologized for
coercing him into coming. "Can we not at least agree to rub
along with some tolerance?" she asked. "I find your bad
humor most debilitating."

He seemed to hesitate, as though he were going to refuse,
and then laughed. His eyes glinted in amusement through
the slits in his mask. "Agreed, Miss Rushforth," he said.
"And you must accept my apologies for being so ill-tem-
pered."

Roberta nodded and felt her spirits rise. "I find it most
uncomfortable to be on the outs with my uncle's colleagues," she said, "and you may rest assured that I will try
not to inconvenience you in the future."

He drew her hand into the crook of his arm and squeezed
it gently. "And I will endeavor not to provoke you," he
replied.

Roberta disengaged herself reluctantly from his grasp
when her partner for the next dance claimed her hand. Afterward, when he returned her to Mrs. Ashley's side, Sir
Nicholas was nowhere to be seen, and she wondered what
he was doing. The supper interval suddenly seemed a long
way away.

A moment later, her hand was claimed again, this time
by someone posing as an executioner.

"A rather macabre outfit to choose," she commented as
he led her into a 'set already forming for the quadrille.

"But I hope 'tis not one you will forget, Miss Rushforth,"
he returned with a smile.

The music started, and they were separated. When he
caught her hand again, she told him he was most ungallant
for exposing her and demanded that he reveal himself. Before he could respond, they were parted once more. The
fragmented conversation continued through the dance, and
Roberta was still none the wiser as to his identity, when he
finally relinquished her to her next partner.

The polka, followed by the galop, left her too breathless
to continue dancing, and she begged the sailor who presented himself as her next partner to procure her a glass of
lemonade. While she waited for him to return, she looked
about anxiously for Sir Nicholas and the comte.

"I'm right behind you, and the comte has yet to arrive,"

Sir Nicholas murmured. "I do hope he doesn't let you down."

"Perhaps it's best he does," she responded smoothly, "for I'm afraid I have worn myself to a frazzle and will be unequal to the task of engaging his attention."

"Then I shall order my men not to dance with you any more," Sir Nicholas said. "It would be a great pity if you failed to accomplish your objectives tonight."

Roberta caught a note of sarcasm in his voice and looked at him sharply. "You mean you have arranged all my partners for me so far this evening?"

Sir Nicholas nodded. "All except for the sailor. I hope none of them have given you offence."

"I—I—really, Sir Nicholas," she began angrily, and then started to laugh.

"Are you all right, Miss Rushforth?"

Roberta nodded. "I was vain enough to believe that my costume was responsible for my sudden surge in popularity. Thank you for protecting me so thoroughly."

He looked down at her and smiled, a warm smile that made her nerves tingle. "There are many disappointed men who are bemoaning the fact that your card is filled," he said. "You do look extraordinarily fetching."

She blushed at his compliment and drew her shawl tightly about her shoulders.

"It's almost time for supper," he continued. "Shall we cast your sailor adrift and claim a table? I've already taken care of Mrs. Ashley and her friend, who are ensconced in one of the anterooms."

"Thank you, that was most thoughtful of you."

They strolled slowly past the revolving couples on the dance floor. Without a word, Sir Nicholas swept her into his arms and waltzed her expertly about the room. He held her close, and for a moment she was lost to everything except the music and his touch. She swayed against him, her eyes half-closed, until her cheek came to rest on his shoulder. She felt his grip tighten about her waist, and instinctively, she pressed herself closer, molding her body to his. Before she had time to consider the impropriety of her actions, the music ended, and Sir Nicholas released her abruptly.

"Shall we make our way to supper?" he asked in a strangled voice.

Roberta nodded, not daring to trust her voice, and followed him meekly to a small room that Lady Winthrop had set aside for her more important guests.

It was the oddest thing, Roberta thought, how she could forget the animosity she felt toward Sir Nicholas, when she was in his arms.

By the time they had reached their table, she had herself in check again and was able to order her meal with remarkable equanimity.

She kept up a flow of chatter as a lackey served them their food, and their new-found harmony lasted until her attention was caught by a tall man in black evening attire. He was pacing up and down the corridor as though searching for someone. From her vantage point, facing the door, she could see him clearly every time he passed the entranceway. Without her realizing it, her shawl slipped off her shoulders as she strained to keep the man in sight.

"I think I've seen the comte," she whispered, oblivious of the look of disapproval on Sir Nicholas's face as he stared at the low neckline of her dress. "To your left, in the corridor."

"Madam," Sir Nicholas growled angrily, "may I ask what possessed you to rig yourself up like a doxy?"

Startled by his tone, Roberta turned to face him. "Good heavens!" she exclaimed in surprise. "I would have thought the answer to that would have been obvious to a man of your experience. I'm certainly not going to attract the comte's attention if I appear demure, am I?"

"If your uncle could see you now, he would be appalled," Sir Nicholas continued. "I'm surprised that Mrs. Ashley allowed you to leave the house in such a state of undress."

"I beg you not to cause a scene here, sir," she responded as calmly as possible. "There are enough people staring at us as it is." She forced herself to smile and placed a restraining hand on his arm, a gesture she hoped their interested audience would interpret as a friendly one.

"You are a woman without shame," he muttered. "I never thought a lady of quality would behave so wantonly."

Roberta tossed her head back and laughed loudly, as

though she found his remark amusing. "Come, come, sir. You certainly didn't give me the impression you were so straitlaced when you ventured into my room at Reigate. I revealed far more of myself on that occasion than I do tonight." She felt him relax slightly, and she laughed again.

"You are, as I have just stated, without shame," he repeated, his voice softening slightly. "You are also incorrigible."

"Ashley has told me the same thing numerous times," she quipped. "Now please, would you engage me in an interesting conversation? The man I believe to be the comte is making his way toward us, and I need a few minutes in which to compose myself for the confrontation."

"I have often thought that the idiosyncratic behavior the majority of Englishmen display when waltzing is caused by the fact that they really abhor that particular dance," Sir Nicholas said obligingly. "Most of them, I fear, prefer a romping polka or a swinging barn-dance, for these are things in which brawn and muscle tell far more than skill. And I believe that the English woman has a weakness for brawn and muscle."

"Really!" Roberta exclaimed. "How very pompous you sound. I have a different interpretation. Allow me, if you will, to pursue the origin of the word idiosyncrasy."

"I'm afraid time is against us," Sir Nicholas murmured, forking some turbot into his mouth. "The comte is approaching."

Roberta followed his example, so that when the comte stopped at their table, they both appeared engrossed in their food.

"My intrusion may seem unwarranted," the comte said, addressing Roberta, "but Lady Jersey assured me that if one wished to make another's acquaintance at a masked ball, it was perfectly acceptable to introduce oneself."

Roberta glanced up, her fork poised above her plate, and inclined her head gracefully. "Monsieur le comte!" she exclaimed, feigning surprise by letting her fork fall to her plate with a clatter.

"Mademoiselle Rushforth?" he inquired, seemingly caught off guard. "Can it really be you? What an unexpected pleasure."

Roberta laughed and put a finger to her lips. "You have found me out," she whispered, "but I trust my secret is safe with you?"

"As safe as it is with your escort," he responded, finally acknowledging Sir Nicholas. "But I must demand a ransom for my silence."

"A ransom?" Roberta giggled. "How ungallant of you, monsieur. What must I do to guarantee your silence?"

"Dance with me," was the prompt reply.

Roberta looked hesitantly toward Sir Nicholas and smiled when he nodded. She pushed her plate away and rose.

"I will agree to just one dance," she said, and followed the comte back into the ballroom.

"Who is your companion?" the comte inquired as he caught her to him. "He seems displeased about being here tonight."

"He is," Roberta confided. "He has informed me that he finds such affairs deadly dull. I cannot think why he accepted Lady Winthrop's invitation. But because of his mood, I don't think I should reveal his identity, for that would displease him even more, I fear."

"I think I know him anyway. He is Sir Nicholas, isn't he?"

"Oh! Please don't let him know you have guessed who he is," Roberta begged. "He—he is so stodgy, he would hate to know that he had been recognized."

The comte looked down at her dress, and Roberta shuddered as she saw his eyes glinting through his mask in naked admiration.

"I'm amazed that he owns to any such scruples," he said, "for the Sir Nicholas I know enjoys all female company. He even pursued my sister until I informed him I found him an undesirable suitor. His reputation, mademoiselle, in certain circles is most unsavory."

"Sir Nicholas!" Roberta exclaimed in disbelief. "Why, I find him to be nothing more than a tedious bore. He is a friend of my uncle's, you know, which is why I am forced to receive him. Do you know him well?"

"We maintain a nodding acquaintance," the comte replied curtly. "Is he on intimate terms with your uncle?"

"An old friend, certainly," Roberta answered. "They play chess together."

"I hope you won't consider my next piece of advice presumptuous," he said, "but if I were you, I wouldn't encourage his advances. He is not a man to be trusted. I am surprised your uncle allows himself to be used by someone of Sir Nicholas's color."

"My uncle enjoys his company. I merely endure it," Roberta said. "But what has he done, precisely, to incur your dislike? I only ask," she added hastily as she felt him stiffen at the question, "because you seem to me to be a man of extraordinary tolerance, and not one to take someone in dislike arbitrarily."

The comte eyed her shrewdly before answering. "Perhaps I will tell you one day, mademoiselle, but not tonight. It is not a very pleasant story, and I see no reason to mar what is left of your evening."

The music stopped, and it was with a sense of relief that Roberta disengaged herself from his grasp. She looked around to get her bearings and finally located Sir Nicholas, leaning against a pillar by the door.

"Thank you, monsieur," she said as she started toward Sir Nicholas. "That was very pleasant."

"May I suggest a stroll in the gardens?" the comte asked. Before she could reply, he had gripped her elbow. "They are very pretty, I am told, and we may just be in time to see the fireworks display."

To her dismay, Roberta found herself being propelled toward the entrance. She experienced a moment of panic until she saw that Sir Nicholas had observed their departure. She nodded her assent. "I would like that," she murmured.

It was an extremely pleasant, mild April evening, and as they left the heat of the ballroom, the night air came as a welcome relief. The well-lit pathways were crowded, and their progress was slow as they threaded their way through the clusters of people who had gathered to watch the evening's entertainment. Pretending to admire the bushes and early blooms, Roberta stopped frequently in an attempt to give Sir Nicholas time to find them, but her panic returned as the comte guided her across a large expanse of grass into a dark, high-hedged area away from the glittering lights. There was no sign of Sir Nicholas.

"We will have an unobstructed view of the display from here," the comte whispered. Roberta shivered as she felt his breath on her cheek. "You are cold, *ma belle enfant?*" he asked in concern. He slid his arm about her shoulders, and she shivered again. He pulled her to him, and the soft caress of the silky fabric of his jacket felt like a snake.

"That's—that's not necessary," she stammered, struggling to free herself. "I'm not cold, really, I'm not."

But she was no match for his strength, and before she realized what had happened, he had pulled her around and caught her to his chest.

"You are so tantalizingly beautiful, *ma chérie!*" he said thickly as he removed her mask. "I find you irresistible." He brought his mouth down to her ear and nibbled the lobe.

Roberta strained against his touch until, with a sickening jolt, she remembered she was supposed to be encouraging him. She went limp in his arms and with the utmost distaste put a hand timidly on his shoulder.

"Monsieur," she said in a breathless undertone, "this conduct is considered most unseemly in England."

His response was to move his lips from her ear to her neck, and to her disgust, she felt his tongue against her skin.

"Please, monsieur, what if someone should come along? Without my mask, I'll be recognized."

"Ma belle enfant, no one will stray this far tonight." His arms moved to the small of her back as his lips sought hers. She turned her head to avoid his kiss, and as she did so, she saw two people approaching. They were quite obviously drunk, for they were weaving a wobbly path and holding each other for support.

"Monsieur," she said urgently. "Quickly, my mask."

He grunted in frustration but complied with her request as he, too, suddenly caught sight of the men. "I must see you again," he said as he tied the strings behind her head. "Will you agree to a rendezvous?"

Her courage returned, now that she was no longer alone, and she nodded. "You cannot have forgotten that I have promised to go for a ride with you on Monday," she said, pouting prettily.

"Indeed, I haven't, but that is not what I meant."

The rest of his conversation was drowned by the two drunks, who chose that moment to burst into song. The words of the ribald ditty were clearly audible, and Roberta blushed.

"I—must be getting back," she said, quickly seizing the chance to flee. "I look forward to seeing you on Monday."

She ran back over the grass, uncaring that the dewy dampness would ruin her satin slippers. She was never more glad to see the familiar figure of Sir Nicholas, standing in her path.

"Your cloak, Miss Rushforth," he said calmly as he held her steady. "I think it is time we departed. We will leave by the side entrance. Mrs. Ashley is waiting for you in the carriage."

She followed him without a word, thankful the darkness hid her agitation. He steered her along a narrow pathway and stopped abruptly.

"I would be grateful if you would refuse any more of the comte's invitations to go cavorting in the dark." His voice cut the silence like a sharp dagger. "You were lucky on this occasion that I had two men stationed outside the ballroom. If they hadn't followed you, there is no saying what liberties the comte would have taken with you, especially as you were so careless as to leave your reticule, with your pistol inside, behind." He removed his mask as he spoke, and Roberta saw the fury on his face.

"Then it's a pity they took so long to come to my rescue," she snapped, "for they were almost too late."

Sir Nicholas reached out, and in one swift movement, pulled off her mask and crushed her to him.

"If it's kisses you seek, Miss Rushforth," he whispered savagely, "seek them from men who don't represent danger."

Roberta felt a sudden surge of anger ripple through her. But before she could think of a suitable reply, his lips came down on hers. She responded to his kiss with a passion that left her trembling, and she cried out in shame when he pulled away. The only sound that punctuated the ensuing silence was Sir Nicholas's heavy breathing.

He started walking again, and Roberta followed blindly in his wake as she tried desperately to compose herself. They had almost reached the side entrance before he spoke again, and then it was to ask her what had transpired between the comte and herself on the dance floor.

In a subdued voice, she recounted the conversation she had had.

"You have done well, Miss Rushforth," he commented. "I doubt he suspects anything, else he wouldn't talk so loosely about his dislike of me. The next time you see him, try to introduce Mr. Lambert's name into the conversation, and watch carefully for his reaction."

"I don't think there will be a next time," she replied through lips that still tingled from his kiss. "I don't think I am equal to the task of persuading him to talk."

Sir Nicholas gave a hollow laugh. "'Tis a pity, Miss Rushforth, that my earlier advice to you on the subject went unheeded. Your decision comes as no great surprise, and it will be my pleasure to inform your uncle later tonight."

Roberta looked at him with loathing as he calmly unlatched the gate and propelled her toward Lord Bromley's waiting carriage. She maintained a dignified silence without difficulty. The events of the evening had so befuddled her mind, she simply couldn't find the appropriate words to express the anger she felt at his callous attitude. She wished she had the courage to retract her decision, but the thought of having to accept any more caresses from the comte was too revolting. Finally, she sighed in defeat.

Williams sprang to attention as they approached, and greeted them in obvious relief. Sir Nicholas extended his hand to help her into the carriage. But, with perverse delight, she allowed Williams to settle her instead. As she sat down, she braced herself for Mrs. Ashley's onslaught about her forward behavior. Instead, in a voice filled with concern, the older woman asked if she were feeling better.

"Sir Nicholas told me that you were taken ill during supper."

Roberta, momentarily stunned by this unexpected piece of thoughtfulness from Sir Nicholas, sighed. "It was the fish," she responded. "I found it to be most disagreeable."

chapter 13

THE NEXT DAY, in an effort to stop her thoughts from straying to Sir Nicholas, Roberta decided to go for a stroll. However, after the events of last night, she felt reluctant to go alone, in case the comte waylaid her, and so she sought out Mrs. Ashley. She finally located her in the library.

"Ah, here you are!" she exclaimed as she peered around the door. "I was certain that you had retired to your room for the afternoon."

With obvious reluctance, Mrs. Ashley put down the book she was reading and looked up. "What is it, Roberta?" she inquired mildly. "I was enjoying Mr. Burns. What a wonderful poet he was. Did you know that he was the son of a farmer?"

"You should talk with Lord Bromley about him, for, if I'm not mistaken, they were acquainted," Roberta replied. "Which poem are you reading?"

"'Ae Fond Kiss.' And what a sad one it is," Mrs. Ashley responded. "'Had we never lov'd sae kindly, Had we never lov'd sae blindly, Never met—or never parted, We had ne'er been broken-hearted,'" she quoted in mournful tones. "It brings tears to my eyes."

"The torments and pains of love," Roberta observed wryly. "Why are you reading that particular poem today, Ashley?"

"I dreamt of you and Mr. Davenport last night. The dream brought to mind that you haven't mentioned him for a while. Are you still nursing a *tendre* for him, perchance?"

"I think not," Roberta responded slowly. "I must confess to some confusion as to how I was able to discern so clearly

111

that I no longer cared for him. You don't know, Ashley, but I saw him privately the other morning." The older woman looked dismayed. "It was something I had to do," Roberta continued hurriedly. "And I'm glad I did, for the meeting proved that you had been correct in all of your criticisms of his character."

"He—he didn't . . ." Mrs. Ashley stuttered in great agitation.

"No, he didn't do anything that embarrassed me," Roberta reassured her, "and I didn't give him any encouragement. Now, please tell me about your dream," she continued. She had no intention of elaborating further on Stephen's visit.

"It was quite dreadful," Mrs. Ashley recalled with a shudder. "Your were at Almack's and Mr. Davenport interrupted the conversation you were having with one of your friends and caused the most frightful scene. He kept insisting that you talk with him. He pestered you all the time. His behavior had all the tongues wagging, and his poor wife sat to the side in acute embarrassment. You were magnificent, though, I'm glad to say, and remained calm and aloof throughout."

"Thank heavens for that!" Roberta murmured with mock gravity. "How did it end? Did I acquiesce or send him on his way?"

"Noooo . . . Sir Nicholas arrived and saw in a trice what was wrong. He intervened successfully." Roberta grimaced at this, and Mrs. Ashley shook her head. "I didn't think you would approve of that. Anyway, he introduced you to Mr. Davenport's wife, Lady Anita, and that put an end to Mr. Davenport's game."

"Is that all?" Roberta inquired, disappointed by the anticlimactic ending.

Mrs. Ashley pursed her lips primly and nodded, but Roberta's suspicions were roused when Mrs. Ashley refused to look at her.

"I believe you're holding something back, Ashley," she accused. "Did Sir Nicholas come to fisticuffs with Stephen?"

"Nothing like that," Mrs. Ashley replied firmly. "The ending wasn't very pleasant, though, and not worth repeating."

"But you must tell me. You simply can't leave me up in the air about it, for that would be most unfair."

"Oh, dear! I don't want to, for you know my dreams often become reality."

"That is why I insist you divulge the ending, Ashley. Forewarned is to be forearmed." She kept her voice light, for she could see that Mrs. Ashley was shaken.

"Well . . . I omitted to mention that the comte was also involved. He was behind Mr. Davenport's hounding of you. He wanted Sir Nicholas to intervene, you see, so that Mr. Davenport would be forced to challenge Sir Nicholas to a duel. I know it doesn't make much sense, Roberta, but dreams are abstract."

"Did Stephen challenge Sir Nicholas?" Roberta asked, frowning at this unexpected twist. "It all seems very fool-hardy and unnecessary."

"I—I was woken before I discovered," Mrs. Ashley said hastily, quite unequal to the task of relating the last gory scene, where Stephen lay in a pool of blood. "Anyway, it was an absurd flight of fancy," she added as Roberta looked at her in disbelief, "brought about, I'm sure, because of my dislike of Mr. Davenport and the comte, and eating too much rich food last night. I wish I hadn't told you of it now, for I can see I have distressed you."

"Nonsense, Ashley. I'm intrigued, that's all."

"Now that I've related my little story, why don't you tell me what you wanted to see me about originally?"

"I had thought to persuade you to come for a stroll with me, but I just remembered I have a few letters to write," Roberta said, suddenly deciding that she should warn Sir Nicholas of the possible danger he faced from Stephen. "Excuse me, dear Ashley, and forgive me for interrupting your dalliance with Mr. Burns."

Much later in the afternoon, long after Roberta had abandoned her attempt to write Sir Nicholas, she impulsively decided to call at his lodgings. She wanted to thank him, anyway, for protecting her from Mrs. Ashley's disapproval last night. The trouble with writing about Mrs. Ashley's dream was finding the right words to convey the possible threat it held. Very few people of her acquaintance really believed that dreams actually could predict the future, even though they all seemed to revel in hearing stories of this type of clairvoyance. Indeed, she might well have held the same skepticism had she not known Mrs. Ashley.

Over the years, Mrs. Ashley had proven to be uncannily accurate in her prophecies, and they had all come to her in her dreams.

But Sir Nicholas, Roberta knew, would be more skeptical than anyone else. He certainly wouldn't put any credence in anything she wrote, so she would just have to tell him personally.

She summoned Polly and asked her to order the carriage for immediate use and to ready herself for an outing.

"We won't be long, Polly, but I need your presence to lend me countenance."

Mystified, Polly nodded, and reappeared ten minutes later with the news that Lord Bromley's carriage was waiting for them.

When Roberta gave Williams her intended destination, he growled his disapproval, saying that it was unseemly for young ladies to visit the lodgings of gentlemen.

"Polly will be with me," Roberta said with some exasperation. "I will be quite safe."

Williams closed the coach door reluctantly, and Roberta sat back, trying to suppress the misgivings about her intended visit. She paid scant attention to Polly, who sat hunched over in her seat, and consequently failed to notice how agitated her maid had suddenly become.

"I know it's not my place to say anything, Miss Roberta," Polly burst out finally, "but I don't think Lord Bromley or Mrs. Ashley would approve of what you're doing. Please let Williams take a message to Sir Nicholas."

Roberta looked at her maid in amazement. "Polly!" she exclaimed. "How dare you! You are quite right when you say it's not your place to say anything. I will forget your impertinence this time, but don't ever let me hear you speak so again."

Polly, quite overcome by these harsh words, started to cry. "I'm ever so sorry, Miss Roberta, really I am," she sobbed. "I don't know what's gotten into me of late. But, you see, the thing is . . . Oh, dear! Would you mind very much if I stayed in the carriage while you got about your business? I just can't face 'im, not now . . ." She broke off as her flood of tears made it impossible for her to continue.

Roberta, mistakenly thinking Polly was referring to Sir Nicholas, looked at her maid in bewilderment until, with a flash of intuition, she guessed why Polly was so hysterical. Then a cold fury enveloped her as she envisaged Sir Nicholas propositioning her maid.

"There, there, Polly," she said in an effort to comfort the girl. "You have nothing to worry about. What has he done to cause you so much distress?"

"No . . . no . . . nothing, Miss Roberta," Polly wailed. "'E—'e thought to enjoy 'imself at my expense, and I wouldn't 'ave any of it. I'm a good girl, really, I am, and if my mother knew what 'e had suggested, she would 'ave turned in 'er grave."

"The monster!" Roberta snapped, her eyes flashing angrily. "How dare he? I'll settle all this for you, Polly, and you'll never be bothered by him again. How dare he be so presumptuous as to make improper overtures to you!" she repeated. "I'll make him rue the day he ever dared to do such a thing."

"Please, Miss Roberta," Polly wailed, "don't 'urt 'im, whatever you do. I—I wouldn't be in such a state if I didn't care for 'im so. But the very idea of 'aving to see 'im again after 'ow we parted, unnerved me."

The carriage came to a halt before Roberta could respond, and, giving Polly a curt command not to move an inch, she opened the door and was on the pavement before Williams could help her.

"Wait for me," she ordered the hapless Williams, all thought of the original purpose of her visit erased from her mind. "I will not be more than five minutes."

She sounded the knocker with a heavy hand, and the door was immediately opened by Jenkins.

"I demand that you take me to Sir Nicholas immediately," she said, brushing past him. Jenkins closed the door with exaggerated slowness.

"I am not certain he is at home," he said. "If you would care to leave your card, Miss Rushforth, I will tell Sir Nicholas that you called." His wooden smile concealed the surprise he felt at Roberta's extraordinary behavior.

"As I have no intention of leaving until I have seen Sir Nicholas, you will be well advised to inform him I am here," she said, removing each finger from her glove with short, deliberate tugs.

Jenkins shrugged in resignation and moved away, but not before Roberta glimpsed the smile that was beginning to spread across his face. Her anger deepened at this display of insolence, and by the time he returned with the news that Sir Nicholas was willing to receive her, her temper had reached its breaking point.

"If you'll step this way, Miss Rushforth," he said, "Sir Nicholas is in his study."

She followed Jenkins quickly and waited for him to withdraw before beginning her tirade. "Sir," she said in righteous tones, "I have borne much from you since you insinuated your way into my life, appearing in my bedroom in the dead of night, involving me with a French comte of despicable character and forcing my companion and me to undertake a journey fraught with danger. Then I knew you to be a man of questionable moral conduct, and later I suspected you of committing serious crimes against the state. But when you betrayed the trust my uncle placed in you, by having the *audacity* to propose a liaison of the basest kind with my personal servant, then, sir, you earned my deepest contempt. No matter what I think of the comte," she concluded, trembling with indignation, "he was correct last night when he called you a man without honor."

Sir Nicholas's reaction was not at all what Roberta expected. His raised eyebrow suggested his surprise at her attack, but the quirk of his lips expressed an amusement that infuriated her all the more. When she saw his smile widen, she became so incensed that she stepped over to him and slapped her gloves across his cheek.

"I refuse to allow you to make fun of me this time," she declared, watching with mixed feelings of satisfaction and dismay as a large red welt appeared on his face. "Unless you give me your word that you will immediately cease your pursuit of my maid, I will inform my uncle."

Sir Nicholas threw back his head and laughed. "My dear Miss Rushforth," he gasped, "I don't know where you got the idea that I've been hounding your maid, but I hasten to reassure you that you have been wrongly informed. Why, I don't even know the girl's name. Now, please, I beg you, take a deep breath to calm your nerves and tell me exactly what has caused your agitated state."

Roberta stared at him, aghast. She could not mistake the sincerity of his words and was mortified by her mistake. "I—I—Oh, dear! I—I must have misunderstood Polly. When she heard we were to visit you, she said she couldn't bear to face you. In fact, she begged me not to come, because she was so upset by the prospect of seeing you again."

"Aha! The charming Polly. Are you quite sure she mentioned me by name?" he inquired, his eyes dancing with laughter.

Roberta shook her head. "I assumed it was you she meant. Who else could it be?"

"One of my servants, perhaps?" he suggested quietly.

As that possibility had not occurred to her, she felt renewed humiliation at the obviousness of his suggestion. It had become a habit, she conceded to herself ruefully, to believe the worst of him.

"I hope you will accept my apologies," she said lamely. "I can't think why I acted so rashly on such circumstantial evidence."

"It's quite all right, Miss Rushforth," Sir Nicholas said gallantly. "Please don't be so abject. It doesn't suit you!"

"But I am truly sorry, Sir Nicholas, and quite ashamed of myself. If you will tell me which of your servants she was referring to, I will speak with him immediately."

"I don't think that will be necessary. I know whom Polly meant, and you must believe me when I say that his affection for her is genuine. If my household were run on ordinary lines, I know he would marry her. Unfortunately, that's not the case, and he doesn't feel that he can offer your Polly a life she would enjoy. Whatever transpired between them is their affair, and I don't think either of us should interfere."

Roberta was surprised by the understanding note in his voice and found herself agreeing with his advice. "It's a pity, nonetheless," she added, "that they can't be given the chance to find happiness with each other."

"I did offer my man employment at Stanway, but he refused."

"You mean so that he could marry Polly? Then why did he decline the offer?"

"On my account, I'm afraid. He has been with me a long

time and will not be persuaded that I can dispense with his services. He's right, of course, for not only is he a trusted servant; he's my protector as well."

"Poor Polly!" Roberta exclaimed. "It's awful how shabbily life treats the lower classes."

"I don't think you need repine, Miss Rushforth. We all get over life's disappointments eventually. Polly can be thankful she has a comfortable position, a charming mistress and a warm bed every night."

"I suppose so. Most women, though, dream of other fulfillments. No matter; as you say, she will recover," she added hastily, not wanting to discuss those "other fulfillments" with Sir Nicholas.

"Now that we have agreed upon that, perhaps you will tell me what prompted you to visit me in the first place," he said. "Has the comte been bothering you again?"

"No, I don't see him until the morning. Actually, I came to speak with you because I didn't think you would have taken anything I wrote on the subject seriously."

"Pray continue. You have aroused my interest."

"Well," Roberta began awkwardly, for now that she had to address herself to the dream, she felt silly. "It's Mrs. Ashley and her prophetic dreams. You see . . ."

"She had one that involved me?" he prompted helpfully.

"Yes. I realize that you might instinctively reject any suggestion of prophecy, but I felt I should warn you. Mrs. Ashley dreamt that Stephen Davenport challenged you to a duel. The comte put Stephen up to it. Mrs. Ashley is convinced that the comte will do everything in his power to harm you."

"I must thank you for the warning. Although, if we are to be honest with each other, we both know that has been the comte's intention since we met in France."

Roberta nodded unhappily. "But I don't think I really believed it until Mrs. Ashley recounted her dream."

"Why do you think your uncle was so reluctant to involve you in this affair?" he asked gently. "The comte is a very dangerous individual and seeks only one thing—the destruction of England. It's my task to see he doesn't succeed."

"Then I'm sure he won't," Roberta replied with simple honesty. "I'm sorry I interrupted your evening. I realiz now that you are abundantly aware of the constant danger facing you." She started for the door.

"Miss Rushforth . . . Roberta." His warm voice arrested her progress, and she turned to face him. "I appreciate your concern more than you realize. I'm afraid that, because of the nature of my work, I haven't allowed myself the luxury of having friends—except for your uncle, of course. I know what I'm doing is right, but it sometimes becomes lonely. Consequently, I live for the moment, because for me, there may be no tomorrow."

Roberta was filled with compassion for him. She knew vaguely how he felt, for she had suffered a similar feeling of isolation in Switzerland. She walked toward him slowly, smiling sympathetically. When she reached him, she stood on her toes and kissed his cheek. "Won't you accept me as a friend as well?" she asked in a whisper. "I would never betray you."

He put his arms about her slender waist and crushed her to him.

"Dammit, dear Roberta," he responded hoarsely, "the trouble is I want more than your friendship."

She looked up at him quizzically and in a detached manner noticed a small scar above his right brow. She touched it gently.

"How did you get that?" she asked.

"I fell off my horse when I was four, and struck my head on a stone. I remember I had a headache for days after."

"It must have been dreadfully painful to have created such a lasting impression," she whispered sympathetically.

"It doesn't compare with the pain I feel now," he said and touched her nose lightly.

Roberta held her breath. She suddenly felt extraordinarily vulnerable. She sensed his need for her yet was uncertain what he wanted, or what he meant by the pain he was suffering at the present.

"Forgive me, my dear," he said, "but there is something I must do."

His arms tightened about her, and he brought his mouth down on hers. She melted in his embrace, unable to fight the desires his kiss awakened. She felt his tongue probing the inner softness of her mouth. She responded, tentatively at first, and then with increased passion when she realized how pleasurable it was to touch his tongue with hers. When he broke away to kiss her behind her ear, she pressed herself against him. Her finger instinctively sought the nape of his neck, and she massaged it lightly.

His hands roamed her body, moving slowly down from her shoulders to the small of her back. He traced the contours of her slightly rounded hips, bringing her to unimagined heights of ecstasy as he did so. Again she responded, and he groaned with pleasure.

When her legs started to tremble, he lowered her gently onto the sofa. She lay unresisting and pulled his face down to hers. They kissed again, slowly this time, savoring the intimacy of the moment. Suddenly she became aware of his hand on her breasts, and she shivered with delight. Then, before she knew what had happened, he moved away.

He stared at her for what seemed to be an eternity, then his cynical laugh penetrated her dazed mind. Before she could stop him, he stood up.

"Lord only knows what madness seized me, Roberta," he said. "I hope you will believe me when I say it will never happen again." He reached down and helped her to her feet. "You'd best straighten your clothes, my dear, before we are interrupted." He smiled ruefully and moved to the sideboard to pour himself a large drink.

Roberta felt a profound sense of disappointment and sadness at his words, not the shame and embarrassment she expected. "Oh, my dear Nicholas, what a futile waste it all seems," she said as she readjusted her dress. "If you won't accept anything else from me, will you at least agree to accept my friendship?" she asked, unable to leave him on such a desolate note.

Sir Nicholas nodded. "Of course," he said with a smile. "Don't look so forlorn, my dear Roberta," he added, "else my resolve will weaken. You will be thankful, one day, that I found my self-control in time."

She laughed shakily and departed quickly, her mind as well as body in complete turmoil.

It was a long time before Sir Nicholas moved. The smell of Roberta's perfume had pervaded the air, and he felt her presence keenly. He filled his glass again and drank deeply.

He had thought himself above falling in love, yet by the time he had downed his sixth brandy, he finally acknowledged he wanted to marry Roberta Rushforth. He laughed derisively at this thought.

When Jenkins appeared an hour later to inquire if Sir Nicholas was ready to eat, he found him sprawled on the sofa in a drunken stupor, the empty decanter by his side.

chapter 14

ROBERTA RETURNED TO the carriage to find Polly weeping uncontrollably. When they finally reached Grosvenor Square, Roberta ordered Polly to bed and told her to stay there for the rest of the evening. And then, deciding to do the same thing herself, she mounted the stairs to her own room.

"Excuse me, Miss Roberta," the butler said when she was halfway up, "Lord Bromley would like to see you."

"I'll be down in a few minutes," she responded wearily, and wished she could refuse the summons. She wasn't ready to face anyone yet.

Fifteen minutes later, after she had changed her rumpled gown and repinned her hair, she found Lord Bromley seated at his desk, reading a dispatch.

"Aha, Roberta!" he said without looking up. "Take a seat; I won't be long."

She sat primly on the edge of a leather chair. She knew her uncle's moods well and could judge from the tone of his voice that he was displeased about something.

The rustling of papers finally ceased, and when her uncle rose and faced her, his expression was troubled.

"I suppose Nicholas has told you of my decision," she said, unable to bear the silence any longer. "I'm sorry if you think I've let you down, Uncle, but the truth is, I find the comte's attentions too awesome. I'm sorry to be so faint-hearted and even sorrier that I refused to believe what you said of him earlier."

Lord Bromley shook his head. "I originally wanted to see you to applaud your decision," he said. "When Nicholas told me of it last night, I felt vastly relieved. However, in light of the disturbing news I have just received from Williams, I'm afraid you have jeopardized your own safety. Why, in heaven's name, did you call on Nicholas this afternoon?"

"I—I—"

"No, don't bother me with petty excuses," he interrupted testily. "The reason is not important; only the fact that one of the comte's men followed you is. In view of your comments to the comte last night that you found Nicholas's attentions an irritation, how will you justify your visit to his lodgings, should the comte ask?"

"I didn't think of that," she murmured contritely.

"Then it's as well for you that *I* did. The comte is not a stupid man, Roberta, and if you see him again, he will find a way to ferret the truth out of you. That is why you will write to him this very minute to say you will be unable to see him as planned. I am sending you to the country for a while."

"But Uncle, I do have a plausible reason for my visit," she said quickly, for although she was unwilling to encourage the comte's attentions, the thought of being banished to Oxfordshire was equally abhorrent. "Really, I do. One the comte will believe without question."

Lord Bromley shook his head. "Don't even waste your breath, for nothing you say will cause me to change my mind."

"Please listen to me," she pleaded. "Can't you see that the comte's suspicions will be aroused if I suddenly disappear? I don't mind seeing him if I'm properly chaperoned."

"Oh, very well!" he said irritably. "Tell me your reason."

"It's quite simple, really. I discovered that Polly was being hounded by one of Nicholas's servants, and I went to put an end to it. Poor Polly was in such a state, her work was suffering."

"Is that the truth?"

"Not exactly, but it will suffice. Oh, Uncle, don't you see? The comte would never question that explanation. In fact, it would please him to think that Nicholas's servants, as well as Nicholas himself, are totally without honor."

He eyed her shrewdly for a moment. "The idea is not without merit, I'll say that much," he remarked in grudging tones. "I'll think about it. But no matter what my decision is, if you behave so thoughtlessly again, I will send you to the country immediately. I simply cannot allow you to create unnecessary difficulties for Nicholas."

"I won't; I promise."

"Still and all, you are not to go for that ride with the comte, even if Mrs. Ashley agreed to go with you. Receive him here, by all means. If he presses for your advice on the horses, take Williams outside with you and examine them in the square. That should be sufficient hint that after his behavior last night, you are not anxious to encourage his suit."

"You are so very sensible, Uncle. I will do as you suggest."

She smiled and kissed him on the forehead. "Good night, dear Uncle. I'll see you in the morning."

As tired as she was, though, sleep evaded her. Every time she closed her eyes, first Stephen's face, then Sir Nicholas's, rose in front of her.

Was the woman who had felt so disgusted by Stephen's offer to become his mistress the same one who had lain on the sofa with Sir Nicholas? she wondered.

By rights, she should be filled with shame for having allowed Sir Nicholas to touch her so intimately. But she wasn't. She had wanted him and would have given herself gladly. Yet what sort of woman did that make her? For she knew that, had Sir Nicholas taken her, he wouldn't have offered marriage.

The answer, she told herself wearily, must be that love was a deeper emotion. And Stephen had defiled the love she felt for him, by his offer. The attraction she felt for Sir Nicholas was not love; therefore, it made it easier for her to accept the fact that she desired him.

"I don't know." She sighed unhappily. "Perhaps, like Sir Nicholas, I lack the ability to sustain a lasting feeling for anyone."

Finally, near dawn, she drifted off to sleep.

It was past ten the next morning before Polly managed to rouse her, and even then, Roberta showed an unusual reluctance to rise.

"The Frenchman will be here before you've completed your toilette, Miss Roberta. And Mrs. Ashley has been asking for you. She said it was urgent."

Roberta lay for another five minutes with her eyes closed and then swung her feet out of bed. "Ask Ashley to come in, Polly, please, and then be so good as to fetch me a cup of hot chocolate."

She sat down in front of her dressing table and was lazily brushing her hair when Mrs. Ashley entered.

"Good morning, Roberta; how are you feeling? I was worried about you, my dear. Perhaps you should stay in bed. It's not like you to be so reluctant to greet the day. You look pale."

"Please don't fuss, Ashley," Roberta begged. She knew her companion meant well, but she was in no mood for chatter. "As I told Polly, I didn't sleep very well. I'll be all right in a while."

Mrs. Ashley surveyed her dubiously for a moment. "Well, if you're certain about that, for there is something most disturbing I must discuss with you. Lord Bromley tells me you accepted an invitation to go for a drive with the comte."

"No . . . no," Roberta interrupted. "I'm not going."

"So I was given to understand. Even so, I can't understand why you didn't mention it to me."

"I didn't mean to offend you, Ashley. I'm sorry if my thoughtlessness has upset you."

"I can only think that you knew I would oppose such a jaunt," Mrs. Ashley continued, heedless of Roberta's interruption, "which I was forced to tell Lord Bromley, in case he thought I had been remiss in my duties. I must insist that you discuss your plans with me in future."

"Where is my uncle?" Roberta asked wearily, unequal to the task of staying Mrs. Ashley's tongue.

"He went out just after breakfast, with someone who looked like Sir Lacey. In fact, I must remember to ask Lord Bromley if it were indeed he." She broke off when she saw that Roberta was paying no attention, and then added with some asperity, "If only Sir Nicholas would be more dogged in his attentions, I'm sure that dreadful Frenchman would be discouraged."

"You are forgetting, Ashley, that Sir Nicholas's interest in me was a sham."

"It's a pity, for I find him to be exceptionally worthy.

I wouldn't have believed him capable of the thoughtfulness he displayed at Lady Winthrop's." She broke off as Polly entered with the hot chocolate. "I'll await you in the green salon," she added before departing.

As Roberta sipped her drink, her thoughts strayed to Sir Nicholas. "Exceptionally worthy!" she mused, and then laughed. "He should feel honored that he stands so high in Ashley's estimation."

She was still thinking about Sir Nicholas when the comte arrived. He was at his most charming, and bent low over each lady's hand.

"Are you ready, ma chérie?" he murmured to Roberta, and frowned when she shook her head.

"I'm—I'm afraid I don't feel well enough," she said. "There was no time for me to send a messenger to tell you of my change in plans. I beseech you to forgive my beggarly manners."

His frown deepened, and he looked at her in disbelief.

"You must blame me, monsieur," Mrs. Ashley interposed. "I have forbidden Roberta to stray far afield today. She has been overdoing things of late."

"I trust you don't hold me responsible for overtaxing your charge, madam."

"No, of course not. If there is any blame, it must be laid at Lord Bromley's door. He kept Roberta up until the small hours this morning."

Roberta shrugged as the comte looked to her for comfirmation. "Then I will have to wait until another day for your advice on the horses," he said.

"Indeed not," Roberta responded. "Such is the shame I feel, I have asked our coachman to join me outside so we can all examine them."

Mrs. Ashley pursed her lips in disapproval but refrained from commenting. Roberta moved to the bell rope and tugged it. Now that she knew she no longer had to endure the comte's lovemaking, she felt extraordinarily calm. Perhaps, she thought, when she talked with him outside, she might introduce Mr. Lambert's name into the conversation. If she were able to report some strange reaction, that would surely prove to Sir Nicholas that she hadn't been completely cowed by her recent experiences.

"You rang, Miss Roberta?" the butler inquired patiently.

"Please ask Williams to join me outside," she said, "and have Polly bring my cloak and bonnet to me."

The butler withdrew.

Roberta smiled at the comte. "Shall we go?" she asked.

He took his leave of Mrs. Ashley and followed Roberta out of the room. "I don't think your companion approves of my company," he said as he closed the door behind him.

"Pay no attention to Ashley," Roberta said. "She's merely worried about my health."

Polly joined them in the hall and helped Roberta into her cloak; then the comte took Roberta's arm and led her outside.

"Do you like the look of the horses?" he asked as his groom sprang to attention. "I think the look is as important as the performance, don't you?"

"I most certainly do not, monsieur," she said emphatically. "Showy horses do not necessarily perform well, and I think the ones you have today will prove my point. Ask your man to walk them a few paces." She paused as the comte issued some instructions to his servant, and then watched as the man led the horses down the road. Williams joined her and stood awkwardly to one side as she suggested, "Why don't you bring them back, Williams, and get a feel of them yourself?"

He grunted and moved away.

"Although, monsieur," she continued, "I can tell by the way your coachman is handling them that they have hard mouths, and will prove difficult to control."

"And I was convinced you would agree with me," the comte murmured.

"But that would have been most unfair of me," she protested. "You did ask me to give an honest evaluation, didn't you?"

The comte nodded. "It is sometimes easier, though, for one to pretend to feelings one doesn't really have."

"Really, monsieur! If that is what you believe, then I am surprised you asked me for my opinion."

"Please don't take offense, Mademoiselle Rushforth. Most women of my acquaintance are not so forthright. And I am glad I asked you for your advice. I will inform Sir Geoffrey that I'm not interested in purchasing his roans, after all."

"A wise decision," Roberta replied. "I know of some other horses that will suit you. I also happen to know that, if you make an offer for them now, you will be able to get them for a reasonable price."

"You interest me. I have not heard of such a team to be had in London."

"The animals I refer to are not to be found here—yet. An old and dear friend of my uncle's died recently in Yorkshire, and as executor of the estate, my uncle is putting the entire stables up for sale."

"How do I know that these beasts will suit me?" he asked curiously.

"Ask anyone you wish what they think of Mr. Lambert's horses," she responded airily. "He was well known in London for keeping one of the best stables in England."

She watched him closely as she spoke and thought she saw his eyes narrow in speculation for a fleeting second.

"A Mr. Lambert, you say? I don't think I ever had the pleasure of meeting him."

He sounded thoughtful, and Roberta pressed on, determined now to shake his confidence. "That does surprise me," she said casually, "for he was quite a gadfly in his day. Indeed, he was proud of the fact that he never missed an important social function."

"I said I had never met him," the comte interposed quickly. "But now that you mention it, I do believe I recall his name being spoken by Lady Jersey. A gambler, wasn't he?"

Satisfied that she had at least forced him into making that admission, Roberta merely nodded. "He certainly enjoyed the dubious pleasure provided by card games. However, be that as it may, would you like me to inform my uncle that you are interested in seeing the horses? They will be in London next week."

"Indeed. You are most kind. Perhaps you will be well enough to ride with me then?"

Roberta laughed nervously and shook her head. "I have no wish to offend you by my lack of interest in your horses. It's just that my uncle wouldn't approve of my venturing so far afield unchaperoned. Indeed, after yesterday, I am most anxious not to overset him further, in case he does as he threatened and sends me to the country."

"After yesterday?" he questioned with obvious interest. "What did you do to give Lord Bromley such offense?"

"I—I—nothing, really. But sometimes he can be a stickler for convention."

"You can tell me what you did, Mademoiselle Rushforth," the comte said. "You know I won't be shocked."

"If you must know, I discovered that my maid was being hounded by one of Sir Nicholas's servants. The poor girl was in tears and didn't know what to do."

"So you decided to visit this man at Sir Nicholas's lodgings?"

There was a note of incredulity in his voice that Roberta ignored. Instead, she nodded firmly. "I know it's not the thing one normally does, but I could not stand by and let Polly suffer. And I'm pleased to say that my call wasn't in vain. It was unfortunate for me, though, that my uncle called for carriage before I returned, else he would never have known about what he termed my 'distressing escapade.'"

"I'm glad you told me about it," the comte said quietly. "You see, I was walking down Albemarle Street yesterday and saw you leave Sir Nicholas's lodgings. I was surprised, as you can well imagine. Especially after what you had told me about your feelings toward Sir Nicholas. Your visiting him didn't make any sense at all."

Roberta's reaction was to recoil, as though shocked by the implication of his words. "I should think not!" she declared. "Why, I didn't even inquire whether he was at home, for the only thing on my mind was to insure that his man ceased his pursuit of poor Polly."

"Did it not occur to you that Sir Nicholas might have instructed his servant to form that particular connection?"

"What on earth could he hope to gain by such a move?" she exclaimed. "No, monsieur, I would never consider that a possibility."

The comte smiled knowingly, which Roberta didn't like it at all.

"You think I'm being silly?" she asked.

"No, no, ma chérie. It's just that I can see exactly what Sir Nicholas would hope to gain by such a move. But let us say no more about it. You have resolved your domestic crisis in a most resourceful way, and I commend you."

Roberta relaxed slightly and beckoned to Williams.

"What is your verdict?" she asked.

"They're as mealy-mouthed a pair as you are likely to find," Williams responded disdainfully. "I wouldn't want them in my stable."

"Mademoiselle's sentiments exactly," the comte said. "Please accept my thanks for the trouble you have taken." He pressed a coin into Williams's hand, not realizing that his action insulted Williams, and turned his attention back to Roberta. "I will bid you a reluctant farewell, mademoiselle, and look forward to the next time we meet."

"Perhaps that will be at Lady Carmichael's," Roberta suggested quickly in an effort to hold his attention. She didn't want him to see the look of outrage on Williams's face. /

"Unfortunately, no, mademoiselle. I shall be out of town. However, I will definitely return in time to see the horses you spoke of earlier."

Roberta allowed a look of disappointment to flit across her face, but, in truth, she was surprised at this piece of information and wondered if Sir Nicholas knew. With a dainty shrug, she said, "Then I will not bother to keep a dance open for you."

"But I will insist on standing up with you twice the next time we meet at a rout, which I hope will be Lady Devonshire's, next week." He moved closer. "Have you given any thought to what I asked you at Lady Winthrop's?" he whispered.

Roberta, taken aback by the directness of his question, bowed her head demurely. "I daren't, for the present," she murmured. "If my uncle discovers I have agreed to a secret rendezvous, he will not hesitate to banish me from London."

"I am content to bide my time, ma chérie," he responded. "We will manage to be alone eventually; of that I'm certain."

The confidence with which he spoke caused her to feel some concern, but she forced herself to look at him and smile.

"I do hope so."

chapter 15

MRS. ASHLEY MAINTAINED a disapproving silence throughout luncheon, and Roberta did nothing to break it. Indeed, she was thankful not to have to bear with her companion's chatter, for she was thinking about what she had learned from the comte. It was really too exasperating not to know what was happening. She drummed her fingers idly on the table, which drew a sharp rebuke from Mrs. Ashley.

"Dear Ashley," Roberta cajoled. "Please don't be in such a taking. I know you don't like the comte, but I can't believe my actions this morning warrant the strong reaction you are now displaying."

"If you continue to behave in such a fast and loose manner, Roberta, I'm afraid I'll have to recommend to Lord Bromley that we leave London for a time. I refuse to be subjected to any more visits from the comte. I find his presence quite terrifying."

Roberta ran round the table to Mrs. Ashley and hugged her tightly.

"The truth is, Ashley, I'm just as frightened as you are. However, I keep thinking of your dream, and I'm certain the comte will do something dreadful to Sir Nicholas if I sever my connection with him too abruptly."

Mrs. Ashley sighed unhappily. "Dearie me, I wish I had never told you of it. I'm so afraid nothing good will result if you continue to see that man."

"It won't be for much longer, Ashley. Anyway, he is going out of town for a while, so we will have a little time in which to recover before we see him again."

"Then I suppose I must be thankful for that small mercy."

She sighed again and pulled nervously at the fringe of her shawl. "If you don't mind, Roberta, I will retire to my room. Maybe a rest will restore my spirits."

Roberta watched her go and then picked at the remains of her food. She wasn't in the least bit hungry but was at a loss to know what to do to occupy her mind. She noticed that outside, the sunny sky had clouded over, and it was now raining steadily. At least the spring flowers were getting a much-needed soaking.

She knew she ought to visit some of her friends, for the pile of invitations increased daily. Yet it seemed almost indecent to resume her normal social life while Sir Nicholas faced such danger from the comte. But the idea of spending another afternoon in fruitless contemplation of her future was also unappealing.

A discreet cough interrupted her reverie, and she looked up to see Perkins hovering in the doorway.

"Sir Nicholas is here, and would like to have a word with you."

"I—I—eh, please ask him to join me. Perhaps he would care for something to eat."

A few minutes later, Sir Nicholas appeared, and Roberta silently gestured for him to take a seat opposite her. She felt momentarily overwhelmed by his presence and didn't dare trust her voice to speak.

"This is most kind of you, Roberta," he said. "I have been so busy all morning, I forgot to eat."

"I—it's my pleasure. There is plenty of food, as you can see. Our chef is of the firm opinion that Mrs. Ashley and I need fattening up, and always presents us with an embarrassing number of dishes." She looked at him as he filled his plate, and marveled at his nonchalant attitude. He didn't appear to be suffering any discomfort as a result of their last meeting. She wished she could be as casual.

He glanced up, and they stared at each other as though transfixed, until Sir Nicholas abruptly turned his attention back to his plate.

"I really came to see Lord Bromley," he remarked at length. "Perkins tells me he left the house early this morning. You don't, by any chance, know where he went?"

Roberta shook her head, still feeling shaken by the

emotions that one look had roused in her.

"No matter," he continued. "I shall undoubtedly track him down at his club later this afternoon."

"Has something happened to cause you concern?" she asked.

Sir Nicholas laughed. "Far from it, Roberta. I have only good news to impart. I believe we are nearing the end of the affair."

"How—how wonderful," she exclaimed. "You must be pleased that you have managed to resolve your problem so quickly."

"Do I detect a note of pique in your voice, that I have managed without your help?" he teased.

"That is an unfair comment, Nicholas, for you cannot be certain that you would have managed to decipher that list without my aid."

"Touché, Roberta, touché. You have been invaluable, and I am only sorry that our paths didn't cross sooner." Roberta blushed at the inference. "Now, tell me how you fared in your interview with the comte this morning."

She shrugged. "It passed uneventfully. He decided against buying the roans, but I managed to interest him in Mr. Lambert's horses."

"Did you, by George! Well done!" he exclaimed, a gleam of interest in his eyes. "Did he acknowledge he knew Lambert?"

Roberta related what had transpired, and then, as an afterthought, added that the comte was leaving Town for a while.

"You are a truly courageous woman, Roberta," he said in admiring tones, "and I'm indebted to you for the last piece of information, for it confirms my own findings."

"Will you not tell me what it is all about?" she inquired. "If you don't, I shall be in a constant state of worry over my uncle's safety. I'm convinced his absence today is in some way connected with the comte's imminent departure from London. It is just a feeling, but one I can't shake."

Sir Nicholas eyed her speculatively for a moment. "You are worrying yourself unnecessarily," he said, "for if that were the case, I'm sure your uncle would have gotten word to me."

"There might not have been time, Nicholas. Ashley said he left in a hurry this morning, in the company of a young man. Someone by the name of Lacey, I believe. Sir Lacey?"

"Good Lord!" Sir Nicholas exclaimed, and put his knife and fork down with a clatter. "What time was this?"

There was an urgency to his question that alarmed Roberta. "It was before ten o'clock. Perkins will know. Shall I call him in?"

Sir Nicholas stood up and started to pace the floor, a worried frown creasing his brow. "Not for the present," he muttered. "I want time to think."

He resumed his pacing, and Roberta's agitation increased. "Who is Sir Lacey?" she inquired. "Why should mention of his name upset you so?"

"Lacey Stigmore works in the Foreign Office—"

"And his name was on that list," Roberta interrupted.

Sir Nicholas nodded. "He has also been invited to attend a gambling party tomorrow night, at a house the comte has hired in Richmond. Now I can't let him attend for his life might be in danger if the comte hears he visited with your uncle. Damn, I'll have to think of another way to penetrate that house." He seemed oblivious to Roberta's presence as he wrestled with this latest problem.

"I don't recall seeing that wretched knife sharpener outside when I rose," she offered timidly, "so mayhap the comte will not know of Lacey's call."

Sir Nicholas swung round and smiled. "You're right, my dear, and thank you for noticing his absence. My plan may still work."

"But I'm concerned about my uncle's safety," Roberta said with a touch of exasperation. Her ignorance of what was happening, coupled with Sir Nicholas's mercurial mood, caused her to speak sharply. "Nothing you have said has convinced me he is not in danger."

A commotion in the hallway caused her to break off, and when she recognized her uncle's voice, she sprang out of her seat.

"Thank heavens he's here," she said, and hurried out to greet him. Sir Nicholas followed, a grim expression on his face. "Uncle, I've been so worried about you!" she exclaimed. "Are you all right?"

Lord Bromley stopped in the midst of taking off his rain-drenched cape and nodded. "Of course I am, Roberta." He caught sight of Sir Nicholas. "Ah! There you are, Nicholas. Come into my study; I have some bad news to impart." He flung his cape at the footman before moving off to his study.

"You'd best retire for a while," Sir Nicholas murmured to Roberta as he passed her. "Your uncle is obviously in no mood to be fussed over."

"Indeed I will not," she responded indignantly. "If something has gone wrong, I want to know about it." She followed him down the short passage and entered her uncle's study hard on his heels.

"Shut the door, Nicholas," Lord Bromley said. He was staring out of the window and didn't notice Roberta. Sir Nicholas obeyed the command.

"Tytler Edwardson committed suicide last night," Lord Bromley said, his voice heavy with grief. "Lacey discovered his body this morning after he had received a note from Tytler. In actual fact," he added bitterly, "it was more of a confession of how he had allowed himself to be used by the comte."

"Oh, no!" Roberta exclaimed, thoroughly shaken by the news. "His name was on the list, wasn't it?" She put her hand on Sir Nicholas's arm, instinctively seeking what comfort he could offer, and stared blindly down at the blue carpet. "He was such a good friend of ours."

Lord Bromley swung round and stared at Roberta in consternation. "Whatever are you doing here, my girl? I had not intended to break the news to you so cruelly."

She blinked back the tears that had gathered in her eyes. "I—I—Oh, Uncle! I was concerned about you." She rushed over to him and kissed him gently on the cheek. "Where, oh where is it all going to end?"

Lord Bromley held her briefly and patted her head lightly. "We will miss him, won't we? However, we shall have to bear his loss bravely. Reality is, Roberta, that the world is a cold, hard place."

Roberta sniffed and nodded mutely. She looked across at Sir Nicholas and wondered if his death would come next. She shuddered at the thought and clung to her uncle for support.

Sir Nicholas, as if understanding the cause of her grief, shook his head and smiled reassuringly. "I give you my word, Roberta, that no more of my colleagues will die."

"I—I trust you," she whispered. "And thank you."

"The time has come, don't you think, John, when the comte's hand must be forced?" he asked. His voice was hard. "Did Lacey tell you he has been invited to Richmond tomorrow evening?"

"Aye, Nicholas. It is obvious that the comte is ready to snare Lacey and extract what information he can. Though Lord only knows what Lacey can offer in the way of state secrets. He hasn't been with the Foreign Office long enough to acquire any knowledge of substance."

"Perhaps the comte seeks to recruit his services, as he did Tavistock's and Stephen Davenport's."

"Stephen!" Roberta exclaimed. "Surely not. I can't believe he would behave so treacherously." She moved to the window. What an incredible fool she had been!

"There, there, my dear," Lord Bromley said. "I thought you deduced that fact from the talk you had with him. He as good as told you, didn't he?"

"I—I suppose so," she said miserably. "Even so, it's difficult to believe. I have been silly, haven't I?"

"No, Roberta, you have been extremely loyal," Sir Nicholas said. His voice was warm, and she smiled at him gratefully. "John," he continued, "it has just occurred to me that we will need Roberta's help one more time."

Lord Bromley frowned. "Explain yourself."

Roberta stared at Sir Nicholas in horror and shook her head. "I don't think I could ever face the comte again," she said. "I could never be civil to that serpent, knowing he was responsible for Tytler's death."

"You mustn't let your emotions sway you, Roberta," Sir Nicholas said, and joined her at the window. He put a hand on her shoulder and squeezed it gently. "We need your help more than ever now."

"I—I don't understand."

"The next time you see the comte, you are going to have to talk about Tytler. You are going to tell him that you saw Tytler the day before he died and that Tytler told you he had made certain preparations, in writing, to atone for his inexcusable behavior."

Comprehension dawned on Lord Bromley's face, and he nodded his approval.

"To what avail?" Roberta asked, gallantly trying to hold back more tears.

"As I said before, the time has come when the comte's hand must be forced. If he knows Tytler wrote a full confession, he will not rest until he has it. Am I right in assuming, John, that it exposes him for what he really is?" Lord Bromley nodded. "And if we detain him, once he has it in his possession, will that not be sufficiently incriminating?"

Again Lord Bromley nodded, a gleam of satisfaction in his eyes.

"But I have no idea when I will see him again," Roberta said helplessly. "It may not be until next week, at Lady Devonshire's."

"He will be back sooner than you think," Sir Nicholas avowed, "for I happen to know he is in urgent need of a fast team. Your mentioning Lambert's horses, Roberta, will entice him to visit you again in the very near future." He glanced over to Lord Bromley, and then added, in a voice charged with emotion, "We are depending on you to help us once more, Roberta. I know you won't let us down."

It was his use of the "us" that charged her courage, and she smiled tremulously. "Couched in those terms, Nicholas, I will endeavor to play my part to the end."

"That's my girl." He laughed and touched her cheek gently before moving away. "It will be interesting to hear what Lacey has to report on the methods the comte uses to induce our colleagues to talk."

"It will be more interesting to see how the comte's attitude changes when he discovers that Lacey has in his possession the letter from Tytler," Lord Bromley responded. "The next few days are going to be very interesting indeed." He chuckled in delight. "Now, about tomorrow night. Ashley reminded me of the Carmichaels' drum. I'm of a mind to escort Roberta and Mrs. Ashley. And I want you there as well, Nicholas."

Roberta's surprise was evident, for Lord Bromley seldom made the effort to attend social functions. "How perfectly delightful," she murmured. "To what do we owe this special treat?"

"Visibility is all-important at this stage, my gal. Some

crony of the comte's is bound to be present, and word will undoubtedly filter back to him that both Nicholas and I were enjoying ourselves enormously, and behaving as though we hadn't a care in the world. That knowledge will keep him off guard a while longer."

Roberta nodded. "It's the same strategy you use when you play chess with me," she said. "Do you promise to play one hand of piquet with me?" she asked.

"Indeed not. I shall be content to sit to one side and watch your admirers make cakes of themselves."

"I'm a little too old to be so besieged, Uncle."

"Then I can see I shall have to act the gallant," Sir Nicholas said lightly. "Would you agree to accept me as a partner, Roberta?"

She detected a note of pleading in his voice and looked away in confusion. "Of course," she murmured. "It will be my pleasure."

chapter 16

WHEN LORD BROMLEY put his mind to it, he could be exceedingly jovial. And as he entered lady Carmichael's, with a lady on each arm, it was apparent to all the onlookers that he was enjoying himself enormously.

Stephen Davenport was standing beside his wife when he first observed the trio being greeted enthusiastically by their hostess. He drew his breath in sharply. It was the first time he had seen Roberta since their confrontation, and he felt an uncontrollable anger as he watched her animatedly parrying her uncle's teasing. It was apparent she did not regret her decision to turn him away. He was suddenly filled with an ugly determination to humiliate her publicly. Excusing himself from his wife, he left the room before Roberta could see him.

Lady Anita sighed unhappily and clutched her fan tightly. She, too, had seen Roberta. She bit her lower lip nervously. By now, she was familiar with the signs of Stephen's black moods and knew instinctively that Roberta's presence was responsible for her husband's abrupt departure. A premonition that something dreadful would happen if they stayed at the drum seized her, and she hurried after him to try to persuade him to leave.

Unfortunately, an old acquaintance stopped her before she reached the door, and by the time she had finished exchanging pleasantries, Stephen had disappeared.

Roberta, blissfully unaware of the small drama that had taken place, took a seat between Lord Bromley and Mrs. Ashley and looked about her with lively anticipation.

"Good heavens!" Lord Bromley exclaimed. "Is that Sally

Jersey over there? My, my, I nearly didn't recognize her. Whatever is she sporting on her head?"

Roberta laughed. "Dear Uncle, you are so behind the times when it comes to the latest fad. That is a peruke. Fashion demands that its color differ from the wearer's own hair."

"Well, in my opinion, it's more suited to a lady of leaner years," he retorted. "I've never seen anything so ridiculous. What do you think, Ashley?"

"She is quite the arbiter of fashion," Mrs. Ashley murmured. "Mayhap it will catch on. Although I myself would never dare wear one."

Lord Bromley struggled to his feet. "Excuse me, ladies, but I can't let this go by without comment. I must pay my respects to Sally."

"Oh, dear! I do hope he doesn't offend her," Mrs. Ashley muttered. "She can be quite abominable if she thinks someone is bamming her."

"She will adore anything my uncle has to say," Roberta responded.

"Of course, of course. She has always been very fond of Lord Bromley. 'Tis easy to see," Mrs. Ashley continued, changing the subject, "that Lady Carmichael has used the 'red book' for her guest list. Every name in it appears to be here tonight."

"I heard someone remark that Lady Carmichael swears on Burke's Peerage the way others swear on the Bible," Roberta said with a chuckle. "It would be interesting to know how many of her guests she actually knows."

"Not many, I'll be bound," Mrs. Ashley said.

"Which is why everyone seems so jolly and gay."

But Mrs. Ashley's attention had been claimed by a friend, and Roberta's last observation went unheeded as her companion walked away.

"So everything appears so very jolly to you, does it Roberta?"

She spun round in her chair as she recognized the voice. "Stephen!" she gasped. "I had not expected to see you here. Indeed, one is always surprised to actually meet an old friend at such a gathering."

Stephen slid into the seat so recently vacated by Mrs.

Ashley and smiled unpleasantly. "Then let us make the most of our time before we are interrupted," he said.

"Really, there is nothing I can think of to say that would be of interest to you, Stephen. Is Lady Anita with you tonight?"

"Her presence will not stay my tongue," he responded acidly. "She has at last begun to realize that she has to obey me. She will not dare move from her seat until I am ready to escort her home."

"Please, Stephen, I cannot like it when you speak so," Roberta said. "And I'm quite certain Lady Anita would be mortified to hear you talk so scathingly."

"'Tis a pity you didn't show more consideration for my feelings at our last meeting. I will never forgive you for that, Roberta."

"For goodness' sake, don't make a scene, Stephen. Remember where we are, I beseech you. You are attracting a good deal of attention already." She looked about the room as she spoke. Her uncle was still engrossed in his conversation with Lady Jersey. Mrs. Ashley was nowhere to be seen.

"I care nothing for the embarrassment I cause you," Stephen replied. "In fact, it pleases me immensely to see you put to the blush."

Roberta, never having been the target of such hatred before, was nonplussed by the venom in his voice. "Really, Stephen," she admonished, "I hardly think Lady Carmichael will appreciate your causing such a disturbance. Please leave me alone."

She spoke urgently, for she was suddenly gripped by a fear that Sir Nicholas would arrive and try to intervene.

The pianist came to the end of his program before Stephen could continue to torment her, and he stood up to acknowledge the polite round of applause. Roberta rose, too, and quickly seized the opportunity this distraction provided to join her uncle.

Stephen stared after her, his top lip raised in a sneer. There was still plenty of time in which to humiliate her.

Roberta greeted Lady Jersey and her uncle breathlessly, and with a forced smile accepted Lady Jersey's compliment on her dress.

"Would you mind excusing my uncle?" she added distractedly. I must speak with him for a moment."

"Take him away, Roberta, by all means, for I declare, my head is spinning from all the compliments he has paid me."

Lord Bromley laughed. "But I meant every one of them, Sally," he declared. He took Roberta by the arm and steered her to a quiet alcove. "You look quite pale, my dear. What has overset you?"

"Stephen tried to cause a scene," she whispered. "I'll be all right in a minute."

Lord Bromley looked at her in concern. "The devil, he did! Where was Ashley?"

"She left my side to speak to an acquaintance, and suddenly he was there. Oh, Uncle, if only I had listened to what you said about him years ago."

"Let us not dwell on him any longer, and instead go in search of Nicholas," Lord Bromley said. "I saw him arrive a few minutes ago, and if we are to still the malicious tongues of the people who witnessed your conversation with Stephen, Nicholas must fawn over you like a veritable popinjay."

"Was a man ever so poorly used?" she responded wryly.

"Never mind," Lord Bromley said. "In another week, you will be able to reject Nicholas's advances and will be free to enjoy what is left of the Season."

Roberta's spirits sagged a little at this unwelcome suggestion.

"Ah! There's Nicholas." Lord Bromley raised a hand in salute, and Sir Nicholas strolled over to them.

"Good evening, Roberta, John. I'm sorry I'm late, but my meeting with Lacey took longer than I expected."

"He knows what to do?" Lord Bromley asked softly.

Sir Nicholas nodded. "And he will endeavor to discover exactly what information our colleagues have passed on to the comte. He will present himself at Grosvenor Square tonight, to report his findings."

"Good, good," Lord Bromley replied. "I have a feeling we will be well served by Lacey." He broke off as several people passed them. "I think we should enjoy what is left of the evening, don't you? Take Roberta in to supper, Nicholas, and lavish attention on her. Keep Davenport at arm's length. Roberta will explain why." He relinquished his hold on his niece's arm. "I'll go in search of Mrs. Ashley, and mayhap we will join you."

Roberta stood awkwardly at Sir Nicholas's side, feeling unaccountably embarrassed by her uncle's presumption that Sir Nicholas wanted to eat with her.

"I will understand if you have made other arrangements for supper," she said.

Sir Nicholas remained silent, frowning at Lord Bromley's retreating figure. After a moment, he turned to her and gave her a penetrating look. "Why are you so anxious to be rid of my company?" he asked.

"You misunderstand me, Nicholas. I will be grateful for any protection you can give me tonight, but any attention you show me will be misconstrued by a large number of people present. I just thought you would wish to avoid being the object of such gossip. My uncle doesn't understand that."

"You are leaving something unsaid. What is the true reason for your agitation? Are you afraid Davenport will cause a scene?"

Although he quizzed her calmly, his eyes reflected his concern. Roberta looked away in confusion. His solicitude unnerved her, and she found it impossible to voice the fears she had for his safety.

"It's Mrs. Ashley's dream, isn't it?" he pressed, and nodded his understanding when he felt her shudder. "Please, I beg of you, don't be uneasy on my account. I will not allow Davenport to mar my evening."

"But you don't understand, Nicholas," she responded, clutching his arm. "He has already caused me a great deal of embarrassment and—and I know he won't let it go at that. He's acting like a man demented."

"Roberta, look at me," he commanded.

She lifted her head and stared at his dearly familiar smiling face. "Yes, Nicholas?"

"Smile, please."

Her lips twitched, and suddenly she was laughing. "I know you are going to accuse me of being melodramatic," she said shakily. "But sometimes I can't help myself."

"The trouble with you, my dear Roberta, is that you read too many works of fiction. Look about you. How many people do you see? Nigh on a hundred?" She nodded. "Then explain to me how Davenport can possibly push his way through the throng and create a stir of any consequence. Now, shall we proceed to the tables and see what delights are awaiting us? Perhaps we can even resume the conversation we were having when the comte so rudely interrupted at Lady Winthrop's. You were, if I remember correctly, about to enlighten me as to the origin of the word idiosyncrasy."

"I was?" she queried. "Oh, yes! In connection with your description of the Englishman's style of waltzing. Dear me, that does seem such a long time ago. I will be delighted to continue that conversation once we are seated." She laughed lightheartedly, and her last vestige of worry dissipated.

Sir Nicholas's benevolent smile hid his deep-rooted concern. He wished he could reassure Roberta that she had nothing more to fear from Stephen Davenport. Unfortunately, the truth was, the man's presence was a constant menace. His own fears for her well-being increased, and he wished now that he hadn't suggested her further complicity in snaring the comte.

The crowds about the laden tables were three-deep. Even so, Sir Nicholas deftly pushed his way to the front, keeping Roberta closely at his side. She watched admiringly, the seemingly effortless way with which he caught the attention of a lackey. He made everything seem so easy, a sharp contrast to the people surrounding them who were still struggling to be served.

"I think this should satisfy our immediate pangs of hunger," he said as the servant handed him two plates filled with lobster salad, ham, oyster patties and game pie. "Follow me, Roberta. I know of a quiet spot where we can eat in peace."

"Have you been to Lady Carmichael's before?" she asked.

"No. I took the precaution of looking over the premises before I joined you and your uncle. There's a small chamber just past the drawing room where we won't be subjected to a lot of curious stares."

"Do you always go to such lengths to insure that your tête-à-têtes with ladies are uninterrupted?" It pained her to think he did, for it served to remind her of his reputation as an accomplished flirt.

"It has become a habit with me," he responded lightly. "My foresight has usually stood me in good stead."

"Which is probably why you have never been discovered in a compromising position," she said cynically.

Sir Nicholas allowed this remark to go unanswered as he shouldered his way into the room. It was empty.

"Pray be seated, Miss Rushforth," he intoned with the formality of a butler. "I can then serve you your meal." He put the plates on a nearby table and readied a chair for her.

"You're impossible, Nicholas," she said laughing at his impersonation. "I find I can't be out of sorts with you for more than five minutes at a time. Your attitude is so nonsensical. Serve me my meal, my good man, immediately."

He bowed low as Roberta sat down, and with a great flourish, spread the finely embroidered chair-back cover over her lap in lieu of a napkin. "I trust this small repast meets with your approval, Miss Rushforth. My kitchen staff toiled through the night, preparing it for you."

She dimpled, having no difficulty in matching his light-hearted mood, then waved airily to a chair on the opposite side of the room. "Won't you please join me?"

"Why, thank you, Miss Rushforth. Your condescension is most gratifying."

"And for goodness' sake, stop addressing me by that name. It makes me feel so old."

He looked contrite and seemed about to apologize when another couple entered. "Even the best-laid plans sometimes go awry. I hadn't anticipated such an intrusion," he murmured. He nodded pleasantly at the couple and sat down next to Roberta. "You were wishing to discuss the origin of the word—"

He broke off as a look of consternation spread across Roberta's face. He looked in the direction of her gaze and swore softly. Stephen Davenport was leaning against the door jamb, staring at them disdainfully.

Nicholas covered Roberta's hand with his own and squeezed it reassuringly. "Pretend an indifference to his presence," he said, "and perhaps he'll go away."

"I think I'll choke if I have to eat anything," Roberta replied. "Please take me away."

"Of course, Roberta." He rose and helped her to her feet. "Although I would like to know what has happened to the forceful young lady who managed, single-handedly, to cower the comte in France."

Roberta smiled and shrugged helplessly. It was impossible to explain why she had changed, for she didn't quite understand it herself.

"Never mind," he continued calmly. "Act as nonchalantly as you can, my dear girl. When we pass him, look up at me and laugh as if in response to something I said."

She gripped his arm tightly, and they moved toward the door. With exaggerated politeness, Sir Nicholas paused by the other couple and bowed. He bid them a good evening and then continued toward Stephen, bending over Roberta as though listening to something she was saying. In reality, he was trying to shield her. Just as they drew level with Stephen, he threw back his head and laughed. Roberta looked at him quizzically for a moment and then joined in.

"I told you it was nonsensical," Sir Nicholas said, "but that really is the way some people conduct themselves."

"I think it quite shocking," Roberta responded. "I would feel mortified if that happened to me."

They had passed Stephen by now, and Roberta breathed a sigh of relief. "And now, if you don't mind, Nicholas, I think it high time I went in search of my uncle and Ashley. Excuse me, please."

"You'd be a damned fool if you did, Sir Nicholas," Stephen said as he swaggered up behind them. "Too many people have excused her from too many things. It's about time she was rightly served."

"You are a foolish drunkard, Davenport," Sir Nicholas said coldly. "This time, I will excuse your behavior, but never again presume to address me in such a fashion."

"What do you know about anything?" Stephen demanded. "She's drawn a spider's web over your eyes, as she did mine. You're the fool, Sir Nicholas, not me. I know her for what she is."

Sir Nicholas's eyes blazed angrily as Roberta tried to

pull him away. "I demand that you apologize to Miss Rush-forth immediately," he said, shaking off her hand. "I cannot allow your insults to go unchallenged."

"Please, Nicholas, it doesn't matter," Roberta murmured anxiously. "He's deliberately trying to provoke you. Take heed of your advice to me. Ignore him, and perhaps he will go away."

"Don't tell me you are going to let her ride over you in such a fashion," Stephen sneered. "Isn't it about time you took a stand?"

"I have taken a stand, Davenport, and I'm still awaiting your apology," Sir Nicholas responded coldly. "Do you make one or not?"

"Your concern for the lady's feelings is quite touching, but I'm damned if I can see why you should be so bothered. She is, as all of London knows, the one who jilted me, and will now, quite obviously, remain on the shelf for the rest of her life."

"Stephen!" Roberta exclaimed in horror. "How can you be so cruel?" She swayed against Sir Nicholas, oblivious to the crowd that had started to gather.

"You had best retract your words, Davenport," Sir Nicholas said quietly.

"What right do you have to demand such a thing?"

"I asked Miss Rushforth, not fifteen minutes ago, to become my wife. That, I think, gives me the right to demand an apology from you." He grasped Roberta firmly about the waist, giving credence to his claim, and smiled at her. "Well, Davenport?"

Roberta returned his smile tremulously, a sudden surge of joy making her heart beat rapidly at the prospect, nay, even the possibility of marrying Sir Nicholas. Almost as swiftly, though, her smile faded as she was forced to acknowledge it had not been a true declaration, merely a ploy to avoid embarrassment to her.

Her spirits sagged, and she wondered how she had managed to delude herself as to her true feelings for so long.

"Do I have to ask you again, Davenport?" Sir Nicholas's voice, clipped in anger, brought Roberta to her senses.

There was only one thing to do, she thought, before the ugly scene turned into a nightmare, and that was to persuade

Sir Nicholas to take her back to Lord Bromley immediately.

"I—I—don't believe you," Stephen blustered even as Roberta tugged at Sir Nicholas's sleeve. "Is it really so, Roberta?"

The crowd seemed to hold its breath as it waited for Roberta's response, and then sighed its disappointment when, instead of answering Stephen, she turned to Sir Nicholas and in a firm, clear voice asked if they could not go in search of her uncle. "And I can only hope," she added, drawing on the last reserves of her strength, "that we will not be subjected to another of Stephen's Cheltenham Tragedies."

Much to her relief, Sir Nicholas nodded. But he gave her cause for further concern when he halted and turned back to face Stephen.

"I will deal with you later, Davenport," he said.

"Please, Nicholas," Roberta begged. "Let us go now."

The crowd parted with some reluctance to allow Sir Nicholas and Roberta to pass, and broke out in excited chatter when they had disappeared from view. Stephen slipped away, unnoticed.

Roberta allowed Sir Nicholas to guide her along the passage. Tears of rage and frustration pricked her eyelids, making it impossible for her to see clearly, although, her mortification at the insults Stephen had flung at her was as nothing, compared to her fear for Sir Nicholas's safety. She was convinced the comte was behind Stephen's deplorable behavior.

Sir Nicholas felt her distress keenly, but wisely did not express his concern. "It puzzled me, Roberta, what attraction Davenport held for you," he said in bracing tones. "I find him to be the most tedious of men."

"He is, isn't he?" she responded in a small voice. "But, Nicholas, I do wish you hadn't compromised yourself so on my account."

"I have done nothing of the sort," he said. "And, what is more, I am still awaiting your acceptance of my proposal."

"I—I cannot. You know that. However, I shall be eternally grateful for your intervention." She gave him a watery smile before continuing. "Please, please promise me you won't seek an apology from Stephen. I'm truly afraid of the consequences."

"I will on the condition that you don't reject my suit, at least for a while. I'm of the mind that we will manage to overcome any gossip if we stay together."

"I don't know what to say," Roberta said unhappily.

"Then I think you should let your uncle decide. Here he is now."

"Good heavens, Nicholas, what is this I hear?" Lord Bromley asked as he hurried up to them. "Some wild rumor has just reached the library, that you have proposed to Roberta."

Sir Nicholas nodded. "And I'm depending on you to persuade your niece to accept," he said with a laugh.

"Well, I have just left Ashley proclaiming to all her cronies that she's not in the least bit surprised by the news," Lord Bromley returned. "So, naturally, I had to pretend an equal lack of astonishment."

"Please, Uncle, say no more for the moment," Roberta begged. "Let us all go home and discuss how we can extricate Nicholas from this situation with the least possible fuss. Stephen forced him into making the declaration, and—and I refuse to accept it."

Lord Bromley glanced at Sir Nicholas in alarm. "Very well, my child," he said gently after Sir Nicholas had nodded. "Nicholas, take her to my carriage. I will collect Ashley and join you outside."

The short journey to Grosvenor Square was accomplished in silence.

Sir Nicholas, who had walked from his lodgings to the drum and consequently was without transport, sat beside Roberta. He glanced down at her several times, as if to reassure himself that she was all right. But that was the only indication he gave of the concern he felt. His face was a mask, although inwardly he was cursing himself for underrating Stephen and allowing such a scene to take place.

Mrs. Ashley eyed the couple with misgivings. She had been overjoyed when the news of the engagement had reached her. Her moment of triumph, however, had been short-lived. When Lord Bromley rejoined her in the library and told her that it was all a gastly mistake, she felt sick with disappointment. There was no understanding Roberta, and she couldn't comprehend why her charge would reject such an advantageous marriage.

Roberta, looking pale and dejected, sat primly on the edge of her seat. She couldn't understand her companion's silence, but was grateful for it. She was acutely conscious of Sir Nicholas's presence and wondered if he already regretted his hasty proposal.

Who could have guessed that her return to England would end in such confusion and unhappiness? It would be so tempting to accept his offer, albeit on a temporary basis, and thus avoid any immediate embarrassment. But could she bring herself to use so noble a man in such a cowardly way?

By the time Williams had halted the carriage outside Lord Bromley's house, she had convinced herself she couldn't. She would accept the consequences of her decision as bravely as possible. If Society shunned her, she could always return to the Continent until the incident had been forgotten.

She allowed Lord Bromley to help her inside the house and stood mutely to one side as Mrs. Ashley bid everyone good night.

"Let us adjourn to the drawing room," Lord Bromley said, "and discuss the implications of this affair in private." He ushered Roberta and Sir Nicholas into the room and closed the door behind him. "I, for one, Roberta, am convinced that you must accept the situation for the moment, no matter how repugnant it is to you."

Sir Nicholas raised his eyebrows at this but remained silent. Although he himself wouldn't have addressed Roberta in those terms, he had to believe that Lord Bromley, with his knowledge of his niece's moods, knew best.

Perhaps if Sir Nicholas had spoken at that point, Roberta would have had reason to change her mind. But his silence convinced her that he was no more willing than she to become embroiled in such an embarrassing situation. Consequently, she remained firm in her resolve to refuse him.

"I don't agree, Uncle," she said gravely. "I can't see whose best interests it would serve. Certainly not mine or Sir Nicholas's. I am prepared to face the consequences of my decision, and I'm certain Nicholas will accept it without argument. Indeed, Nicholas," she continued with a hollow laugh, "I expect you to feel infinitely relieved in the morning that I refused to avail myself of your very kind offer."

"Will you listen to me for a moment, Roberta?" Sir Nicholas asked. He felt an overwhelming admiration for her show of courage and had to fight the urge to embrace her. "With your uncle's permission, I will gladly marry you to avoid causing you unnecessary suffering." His words surprised everyone, including himself.

"Egad, Nicholas!" Lord Bromley exclaimed. "That is most handsome of you."

Roberta had to struggle to check the anger she felt at this humiliating proposal. What right had any man to be so condescending? she thought. Especially one who had yet to succumb to the torments and uncertainties of loving another being. She became aware that both men were looking toward her, awaiting her answer.

"I think a marriage based on pity, Nicholas, would be disastrous," she said with quite dignity. "My answer is no. Now, if you will excuse me, gentlemen, I will bid you good night. You have a meeting with Sir Lacey, I believe, and I'm sure you will want to prepare for it." She left the room with unhurried grace before either man could speak.

"It would seem I have made a mull of matters," Sir Nicholas observed ruefully. "I'm sorry, John. I had no other idea in mind than to ease Roberta's suffering. I realize now how offensive I must have sounded."

Lord Bromley shook his head wearily. "You were nothing of the kind, Nicholas," he said. "Roberta is a wonderful young lady, but headstrong to a fault."

Sir Nicholas laughed. "I liken her to an unbroken filly," he murmured with affection. "Difficult to handle, even if one uses a firm hand. Now, about Davenport, John. Do you give me leave to deal with him?"

"In any way you see fit," Lord Bromley replied. "What do you have in mind?"

"I thought to call him out while everyone is still under the impression that Roberta and I are betrothed. Then, if it should happen that he sustains a fatal injury, we can get by without announcing publicly that he was a traitor."

Lord Bromley nodded. "Just insure *you* don't sustain an injury, Nicholas."

chapter 17

ROBERTA WAS SURPRISED to see a strange young man already seated at the breakfast table. He was listening to Mrs. Ashley with a patient smile on his pleasant countenance even while suppressing a yawn.

"Ah, Roberta," Mrs. Ashley exclaimed as Roberta entered the room. "I'm so very glad you have joined us, for I don't believe you have met Sir Lacey Stigmore. I can't tell you what a delightful surprise it was to see him seated here. He had an early appointment with Lord Bromley, and your uncle insisted he stay and eat with us."

As Sir Lacey sprang to his feet, Roberta inclined her head graciously. She, too, was grateful for this diversion and knew instinctively that her uncle had purposely arranged for Sir Lacey to stay in order to protect her from Mrs. Ashley's questions.

"Sir Lacey," she said pleasantly, "may I say how pleased I am to make your acquaintance?"

"Miss Rushforth," he returned, bowing low.

"Please continue with whatever you were discussing," Roberta said, "while I help myself." She turned to the sideboard and served herself a small helping of shirred eggs from one of the many warming dishes on display.

As Roberta sat down opposite Sir Lacey, Mrs. Ashley urged her to have more. "I declare, you have quite lost the bloom to your cheeks you acquired in Switzerland," she said.

"When were you in Switzerland?" Sir Lacey inquired. "I was there myself several years ago, but unfortunately, only for a fleeting visit."

"And my stay, also unfortunately, was far too long." Roberta laughed, grateful for his timely intervention. She found Mrs. Ashley's fussing too much to bear today. "I was there for six months, undergoing treatment for a lung disorder."

"I am sorry," Sir Lacey responded. "It was nothing serious, I hope."

"No, thank goodness," Mrs. Ashley replied. "The specialists were wonderful, weren't they, Roberta? The sanitorium we stayed in was more palatial than most manor houses I've seen in England. And the service was excellent."

Roberta was content to let Mrs. Ashley carry the conversation. She studied Sir Lacey from beneath lowered lashes and decided she liked what she saw. His firm chin jutted out arrogantly, and his eyes, although red-rimmed from lack of sleep, seemed to constantly assess what he saw. He was not a handsome man, but she found the air of purpose about him attractive. In many ways, he reminded her of Sir Nicholas.

She sighed as the image of Sir Nicholas rose before her, and wondered if she would ever be able to face him again with any degree of calmness.

Roberta was aroused from her reverie by the appearance of Perkins, who coughed discreetly and passed her a note from Lord Bromley requesting her immediate presence. She interrupted Sir Lacey, much to Mrs. Ashley's annoyance, and excused herself.

Lord Bromley looked rumpled, but there was a triumphant gleam in his eyes.

"That young man in the dining room, Roberta," he said without preamble, "is quite remarkable. I hope you treated him with due respect."

Roberta laughed in relief. She had been certain her uncle had summoned her to persuade her to change her mind about Sir Nicholas, but obviously that was furthest from his mind.

"I gave him a withering look when he presumed to engage me in conversation and have just now left him crying in despair on Mrs. Ashley's shoulder," she said gaily. "Really, Uncle, I'm surprised you even ask. It's your shocking lapse in manners that should be questioned. Sir Lacey was nonplussed, to say the least, when he realized you had abandoned him to the ministrations of two ladies."

"Nonsense, my gal, nonsense," Lord Bromley responded jovially. "He must get used to being plunged into unexpected situations. He has to learn to hold his own, to act like a chameleon and take on the hue of his surroundings. Once he has mastered all those arts, he'll go far. Mark my words, Roberta, he'll go far."

"You're very jolly this morning," she teased. "Has Sir Lacey, perchance, managed to solve some of your more pressing problems?"

"If you mean 'has he discovered what secrets have been passed to the enemy?' the answer is yes. And the comte used the oldest ploy in the world, Roberta, to extract these secrets from my colleagues."

"Feminine wiles?" Roberta suggested.

"Yes, feminine wiles. The comte employed a certain young lady of great beauty, known as Veronique, who enticed my colleagues into her boudoir. There, after being administered drugged drinks, they willingly answered all the questions she asked. I can only presume that Lambert and Tytler realized what they had done and, disgraced at being unwitting traitors, took their own lives."

"How did Sir Lacey manage to make this young lady talk?" Roberta inquired, impressed by the young man's discovery.

"By speaking of Tytler. She had no idea he was dead, and was very upset when she heard of his untimely demise. Unbeknownst to the comte, she had made the fatal mistake of falling in love with him."

"Oh, the poor girl," Roberta exclaimed, immediately understanding her plight. "How terrible for her."

"Doubly so," Lord Bromley remarked. "For Lacey is convinced that she had no idea how she was being used by the comte. Her only interest was the money she received. It seems she has an invalid brother who needs expensive help."

"The fiend! Yet it is what one should expect, I suppose. Men like the comte always manipulate the weak. What will happen to her now?"

"We'll take care of her and her brother, as long as she agrees to testify against the comte."

"And will she?"

"I'll know later, when Nicholas returns."

"Will—will her testimony provide sufficient proof?" Roberta inquired, deliberately veering away from the subject of Sir Nicholas.

"If she doesn't falter. However, as I daren't depend on her, it is still imperative that we force the comte to compromise himself." He broke off and stared out of the window, a pensive expression on his face.

"And you still want me to aid you, is that it?"

"Not if you don't want to, Roberta," he responded. "Nicholas and I discussed that aspect last night after you left us. I can find another way, if need be, of informing the comte that I possess Tytler's letter of confession."

"But it would be more expedient if I were the conduit?"

"It would."

"Very well, Uncle. Then you must tell me what I am to do."

Roberta was thoughtful when she left Lord Bromley's study half an hour later, and she hoped his optimism wouldn't prove unfounded. Now there was nothing any of them could do until the comte paid her a call. In spite of Lord Bromley's certainty that that event would occur later the same day, she wasn't at all sure. She couldn't quite believe that the contretemps caused by Stephen would cause the comte to rush back to London to see her.

Lord Bromley was correct, though. Not fifteen minutes after she had left her uncle, the butler announced the comte had called.

"Show him into the front parlor," she said. "I will join him there. Please inform my uncle that he has arrived."

It was a full twenty minutes, however, before she could summon sufficient courage to face him. And it was to her credit that, when she eventually entered the parlor, she looked genuinely pleased to see him.

"How glad I am that you chose such a melancholy day to visit," she remarked. "My spirits are in need of a diversion that only you can provide."

The comte caught her hand in his and lifted it to his lips. *"Mon enfant,* why are you so sad? Could it be that you are already regretting your engagement to Sir Nicholas?"

Roberta started and pulled her hand away. "I had hoped that story wouldn't have reached you," she whispered forlornly. "It's not true, and if Mr. Davenport hadn't behaved so vilely, I could have informed Sir Nicholas that I had no intention of accepting his offer."

"So Sir Nicholas did propose, did he?"

"Yes," Roberta responded. "That I can't deny. Oh! monsieur, if only you had been there last night, none of this would have happened."

"Ma pauvre enfant. Please don't distress yourself. I will stand by you and lend what support I can."

"Why, thank you, monsieur, that is most gallant of you. Although, in my present state of despondency, even that kind offer will do little to elevate my spirits, I'm afraid."

"What else has happened to overset you?" he inquired quickly.

"My depression is caused by the death of one of my friends. The scene last night merely added to it."

"A close friend?" he asked, squeezing her hand sympathetically.

Roberta nodded and allowed the tears that had suddenly welled up in her eyes to flow freely down her cheeks. "Please forgive me," she mumbled into his corded jacket. "It was just that Tytler was like a brother to me."

"Tytler Edwardson?" the comte queried. As Roberta looked up at him, she saw his eyes narrow in a calculating fashion. "I had no idea he was dead," he added. "When did it happen?"

"You knew him?" Roberta asked, feigning surprise.

"Not well," he responded suavely. "We were merely nodding acquaintances."

"Then you can't really know what a sad loss it is. Poor, poor Tytler. And to have killed himself the day after he told me that he had made certain preparations to clear his name . . ." She broke off in distress. "It doesn't make sense, does it?" she whispered.

"I wasn't aware of any slur attached to his name," the comte remarked casually. "Perhaps you misheard him, mon enfant." He walked over to the window and stared out. "What, exactly, did he say?" he inquired casually.

Roberta shrugged and joined him in the recess. She noticed immediately that the knife sharpener was back in his position under the oak tree, and this distracted her for a moment. "I—I can't recall," she said nervously. "I—I assumed he was talking about his ill-fated liaison with Sir Lacey Stigmore's sister."

"I hadn't heard that on-dit."

"Oh, dear! Perhaps I shouldn't have mentioned it. But the fact remains that I don't understand why Tytler saw fit to end his own life, when he had written to Sir Lacey with a full explanation of his behavior." She was watching him intently and was gratified to see a look of alarm flit across his face. "I mean, what shame could Tytler possibly have brought to the Edwardson name that would make him take such a drastic step?" She fumbled in the folds of her dress for her pocket and finally located her handkerchief. She drew it out and, under the pretext of blowing her nose, was able to study his obvious discomfort at her news.

"Have you seen this letter?" he inquired with some urgency.

"No...no, not yet, but maybe when my uncle has it, he will let me read it."

"I don't understand," the comte said.

"When I heard of Tytler's death and told my uncle of the letter, he summoned Sir Lacey here in order to obtain a copy. I believe my uncle wanted to satisfy himself of the true cause of Tytler's suicide."

The comte swore softly.

"Have I said something to concern you?" she asked.

"Not really. It's just that I saw Sir Lacey last night, and he didn't mention anything about it."

"I don't find that surprising, monsieur. He would, I'm sure, be reluctant to discuss it with anyone for fear of inflicting further damage on his sister's reputation."

The comte laughed. To Roberta, it sounded more like a sneer. "Of course, mon enfant. I forgot for a moment how prudish you English are."

"Quite so," she murmured, and moved away, wondering how she could persuade him to go before Mrs. Ashley discovered her alone with him.

The problem, however, was solved by the comte himself

moments later. He drew out his time piece and exclaimed in affected annoyance, "Please forgive me, ma chérie. I must take my leave of you. I'm expected somewhere in a few minutes on urgent business."

"Will you call on me again soon?" she asked.

"I will not allow so much time to elapse before I see you again; that I promise." He walked over to her and taking her chin in his hand, forced her to look up at him. "Au revoir, ma chérie," he murmured.

For a moment Roberta thought he was going to kiss her, and she quickly averted her face. "Please, monsieur, Ashley may join us any minute."

"The day will soon be here when you can dispense with such maidenly concern," he snapped, and was gone before Roberta could respond.

When Mrs. Ashley entered, ten minutes later, Roberta was still standing in the middle of the room. She looked deathly pale, and Mrs. Ashley hurried over to her.

"My dear Roberta," she said. "I have just had a long talk with Lord Bromley and am here to tell you not to worry unduly about the events of last night. He has told me exactly what happened, and I won't increase your suffering by discussing it further with you. However, I want you to know I sympathize with your plight, and will do anything I can to help ease your pain. Would it help if we retired to the country for the rest of the Season?"

"Oh, Ashley, dear, dear Ashley!" Roberta cried, completely overwhelmed by her companion's concern. Tears coursed down her cheeks, and with uncommon meekness, she allowed Mrs. Ashley to lead her to the sofa.

"There, there, my dear," Mrs. Ashley murmured. "Sit down. A good cry will do you a world of good." She cradled Roberta in her arms, whispering endearments all the while.

Roberta's sobbing increased; she was unable to control herself in the face of such gentleness. She clung to Mrs. Ashley, oblivious to everything except her own misery.

Eventually, though, she became aware of Mrs. Ashley's stroking her hair, and she drew comfort from being cosseted like a child. Her crying subsided, and she gratefully accepted the delicate lace handkerchief Mrs. Ashley proffered.

"Dry your eyes, child, and then, if you wish, we can talk."

"There's nothing to say," Roberta responded after she had blown her nose. "Nothing at all." The truth was, though, she wanted nothing more than to confide in Mrs. Ashley. "See," she continued, forcing herself to smile, "I feel much better already. I think I have been wanting to indulge myself in a bout of tears since I discovered my illness was not incurable."

"And a very natural impulse it is, too," Mrs. Ashley responded with such understanding that Roberta was hard put not to cry again. "You have been through so much this past year, I'm surprised you haven't broken down sooner. Now, my dear, I'm going to prescribe a walk in the gardens. The fresh air will do you a world of good, and might even put some color into your cheeks."

Mrs. Ashley's prosaic attitude was all that Roberta needed to restore her spirits, and she nodded her agreement.

"If you don't mind, though, Ashley, I will go and see Lord Bromley first. There is something I want to ask him."

"He went out, my dear, almost immediately after we had concluded our discussion. I believe a note from Sir Nicholas was the cause of his sudden departure. Anyway, before he left, he said he had no idea when he would return."

Roberta frowned. It was strange that her uncle would disappear before she had told him what had transpired between herself and the comte.

"Oh, and I almost forgot, for my head's in such a muddle today, he asked me to tell you that Perkins informed him of the situation regarding Tytler's letter. And he said there was no need for you to worry about it."

Roberta nodded. She should have known her uncle wouldn't have left her alone with the comte without insuring that help was near at hand. Perkins must have been outside the door and heard every word of her conversation with the comte.

"He didn't tell you where he was going, I suppose?" she asked.

"No," Mrs. Ashley said with a shake of her head. "He was in a great hurry, so I can only assume it was something important, for you know he hates to rush."

An uneasiness gripped Roberta which she couldn't shake, and she turned to Mrs. Ashley urgently. "That dream you had Ashley, please tell me how it ended."

"I—I told you, Roberta, I awoke before—"

"Please Ashley," Roberta interrupted impatiently. "You must tell me, especially in light of the events of last night."

Mrs. Ashley shrugged. "There was a duel, and—and Sir Nicholas injured Mr. Davenport."

Roberta's joyous reaction to this disclosure clearly puzzled Mrs. Ashley, and she hastily added that it was only a dream and bore no reality to life.

"You are probably right, Ashley," Roberta responded lightly. "But in this instance, it might well turn out to be the truth."

chapter 18

THE INTRICATELY EMBOSSED envelope that the butler handed to Roberta as Mrs. Ashley was pouring tea aroused her curiosity. It also served to divert her from the interview she had just had with Lord Bromley, which had left her feeling most disgruntled.

"I can't think who it can be from," she remarked, and wrinkled her nose in distaste at the perfume with which the note was drenched. "None of my friends indulge themselves in this latest fad of scenting their missives."

"You'll never know if you don't open it," Mrs. Ashley declared. "Hurry, child, it might be another letter of support in response to your contretemps with Stephen Davenport."

Roberta laughed at her companion's impatience. "I think I will wait until after tea, and spend more time contemplating the many notes I have already received. I thought it was extremely magnanimous of Mrs. Pinson to write, didn't you? I didn't even see her last night." With deliberate slowness, she placed the letter on the table in front of her.

Mrs. Ashley sniffed and pulled a face. "The scent is awful, isn't it? I think you'd best open it and read the contents; then we can burn it and get rid of the smell."

"Oh, very well!" Roberta said, and with a show of reluctance, slit open the envelope. "Why, it's an invitation to join Lady Anita for supper tonight," she exclaimed. "She apologizes for Stephen's behavior and wishes to know how to make amends." She read on a little further and then added, "Oh! Isn't this sweet of her, Ashley? Here, I'll read it to you: 'If you are agreeable, as indeed I hope you will be, for I have long desired to make myself known to you,

I will send my carriage around at seven-thirty in order that we can enjoy a comfortable coze over dinner!"

"I think you should accept," Mrs. Ashley said, "for I believe if you can reach an accommodation with Lady Anita, it will go a long way to silencing the gossips."

"My own thoughts exactly," Roberta said. "Will you join me, Ashley?"

"My company might prove something of an incumbrance, don't you think? If the two of you are left alone, you are likely to talk more freely. Take Polly with you, and I will retire early, for I really am feeling very tired today."

As Roberta dressed for dinner that evening, she recalled her discussion with her uncle earlier that afternoon. The proprietary attitude Lord Bromley had adopted with her still rankled. He had deftly avoided answering her questions about his whereabouts all day, and had laughed heartily when she had mentioned her belief that Sir Nicholas had challenged Stephen to a duel.

"A most preposterous suggestion," he had said. "Why, Nicholas and I are dining together tonight at my club. He would hardly have agreed to join me if that was his intention."

"Are you not concerned about the possibility that the comte might try to take Tytler's letter whilst you are out?" she countered irritably.

"By the same token, my dear, the comte is not likely to attempt to steal the note if he knows I am at home, and since our goal is to catch him red-handed, so to speak, we prefer to encourage rather than discourage him. I can't guess what method he will use to gain entry to my study, but as long as you and Ashley retire early, and keep to your rooms, I do not envisage any problems."

"Well, I do," Roberta said. "And I can't like the idea of the comte being allowed to run free in our home."

"I assure you, Roberta, you will be fully protected. I have replaced the servants with my own men for the night. If the comte does come tonight and tries to take anything but that letter, he will find his way completely blocked."

She had nodded reluctantly, but on receipt of Lady Anita's letter, she hadn't hesitated to change her plans for the evening.

Just then, the front-door knocker sounded, and she allowed Polly to put the finishing touches to her toilette. She looked extraordinarily fetching, in a simple blue chiffon dress caught beneath her breasts by a ribbon of a deeper blue.

Lady Anita's coachman was most solicitous and handed Roberta into the luxurious carriage with due deference, leaving Polly to scramble in unaided. He inquired of Roberta if she was in need of a blanket, and when she shook her head, he folded the fox fur neatly and placed it on the seat beside her. When he had satisfied himself that she was comfortable, he closed the door, and they were on their way.

When the coach came to a halt, Roberta peered out into the inky blackness. As her eyes accustomed themselves to the dark, she frowned. "Where on earth are we?" she exclaimed.

"I dunno, Miss Roberta," Polly said. "It din't look like Portman Place to me, though."

Suddenly the door opened, and a man, muffled, hatted and caped, climbed in. He closed the door quickly. Polly screamed, and the man put his hand over her mouth. Roberta quickly tried to open the door, but the man commanded her to stay seated.

"I wouldn't do anything foolish if I were you, Roberta," he added, "else this young lady might suffer."

"Stephen!" she cried. "Don't be so ridiculous. Unhand Polly this instant and tell me what this is all about."

"So you were really taken in by my letter, were you?" he said, pushing Polly away. "Obviously the comte knows you far better than I thought."

"Is—is he behind this—this abduction?" Roberta stammered, momentarily unable to hide her fear. "What does he want with me? Where are you taking us?"

"Oh, Miss Roberta," Polly interjected in a frightened voice. "What's going to happen to us?"

"Be quiet, Polly," Roberta commanded more sharply than she intended. "I don't think Mr. Davenport will tolerate your hysterics with kindness." Polly slumped back on the seat, a look of sheer terror on her face. "Answer me, Stephen," Roberta continued. "Where are you taking us?"

"So many questions, my dear," Stephen said. "If I tell

you we are going to visit your papa, will that suffice?"

"My papa!" Roberta exclaimed in horror as a terrible realization dawned on her. "I'm afraid I don't know what you mean." She fought valiantly to stem the panic that threatened to overwhelm her. Finally, she succeeded, by forcing herself to think how Sir Nicholas would react in such a situation. "Take me home, Stephen," she said with studied nonchalance. "You know my papa has been dead these past twenty years."

"And it was my duty to inform the comte of that fact," Stephen responded with a sneer.

Roberta felt a surge of anger at his treacherous words, and she struck at him blindly. He caught her hand easily, however, and held in in an iron grip.

"Did you honestly believe the comte wouldn't discover you'd tricked him? What a little fool you were, and what bigger fools your uncle and Sir Nicholas have been."

Roberta pulled her hand free and moved to the far side of the seat, so that she was opposite Polly. She felt more comfortable now that she had put some distance between herself and Stephen, and she relaxed slightly.

"We have not been as stupid as you," she said calmly. "For any man who thinks he can betray his country without being found out lives in a fool's paradise. My uncle will see that you pay for your duplicity."

Stephen laughed. "You are the only one who knows, my dear, and after the comte has had his way with you, I doubt anyone will listen to what you have to say."

"Does that mean you are taking me to his house of ill repute in Richmond?" she inquired.

"Aha, so you know of that, do you? We will go there eventually. But first we have to return to Grosvenor Square and pick up the comte."

Roberta sat bolt upright. If they were to return home, there was a possibility of escape, surely?

But Stephen, as if reading her mind, laughed. "I wouldn't make any attempt to escape, if I were you," he said callously, "for I will not hesitate to use this." He produced a pistol from the folds of his traveling cape and brandished it in the air. It glinted manacingly in the flickering carriage light. "Sit back, my dear, and relax."

Roberta obeyed reluctantly. "You can put it away, Stephen. I won't give you cause to use it." She spoke coldly, for she was determined not to let him see how frightened she really was. "What business has the comte at my uncle's home?" she inquired. "My uncle is out for the evening, and there will be no one there to receive him."

"How perceptive of you, my dear. But that is precisely what the comte wants. A few minutes of privacy in your uncle's study, to find a certain letter."

"A letter?" Roberta questioned, feigning ignorance. "I don't understand. Anyway, I'm sure he will have wasted his time, for the servants will not admit him into the house if no one is there."

"The comte, my dear, is not that stupid. He will be admitted, because he bears a message, supposedly signed by Lord Bromley, summoning him to Grosvenor Square. The footman will have no choice but to invite him in. He will insist on being shown into the study—in fact, that is probably happening even as I speak—he will then conduct a thorough search for the required document. In approximately ten minutes, he will inform the footman that he can no longer wait, and he will leave. We shall be outside, waiting for him."

"You sound very certain of his success, Stephen," Roberta remarked. "What happens if he fails to find this—this letter?" But she knew he wouldn't, for her uncle had shown her exactly where he was going to leave it—on top of his desk, with a paperweight on it. "Why is it so important, anyway?" she added. "What does it contain that he dares take so great a risk? I mean, my uncle might return and discover him in the middle of his search."

"I doubt it, Roberta. For, if I'm not mistaken, your uncle and Sir Nicholas are at this very moment heading for Richmond. They have been led to believe that Sir Lacey Stigmore is there and is in trouble." He broke off and laughed as Roberta gasped in horror. "It is my one regret that I will not be at Richmond when they walk into the trap that has been set for them."

"What trap?" Roberta cried. "What is going to happen to my uncle and Ni—Sir Nicholas?"

"I find your concern for *Nicholas* quite touching," Stephen sneered. "It's remarkable that your own fate, and that of your maid's, doesn't weigh so heavily on your mind. Could it be that you have allowed yourself to fall in love with the man you are about to marry?"

"No—no, it's not true," she cried out, refusing to acknowledge the truth of his words. "It's my uncle's safety that concerns me. He is an old man, and not used to violence."

"Then you should be relieved to learn that Lord Bromley will be released in the morning, when he will be free to return to London."

"And Sir Nicholas?"

Stephen shook his head. "I'm not at liberty to discuss his fate. But as for you and your maid, you will both sail with the comte and myself to France tonight."

Roberta gasped. "Surely you don't intend to take us with you."

"Why not? Your presence will be our guarantee for a safe exit. The comte will explain what he expects from you, when he joins us. And if you're wise, Roberta, you won't disobey, for he has an unpleasant way of compelling people to comply with his dictates."

Roberta stared at him aghast. How could she have underestimated the comte so?

"Is there no way I can persuade you to change your mind, Stephen?" she asked in one last desperate attempt to play on his sympathy. "Are you so lost to all sense of decency that you would refuse to help me escape?"

"Don't play on my emotions, Roberta," he snapped. "I offered you carte blanche when you returned from France, and you refused. Now you must face the consequences of that decision."

"I don't understand you, Stephen," she said. "I thought you loved me. Was that all a lie?"

He seemed to waver, and Roberta was about to press on, when the coach came to a halt outside her uncle's house.

"Damn you, Roberta, be quiet. I made the mistake once before of allowing my desire for you to overcome my sense of duty. It won't happen again."

Tears of defeat flooded her eyes, and she turned her head to hide them from Stephen. She clenched her fists tightly

as she fought to regain control of herself, and glanced out
of the window. Her gaze rested on the oak tree, and for a
moment she thought her imaginaion was playing tricks on
her. She blinked several times to clear her vision and nearly
cried out in joy when she recognized Davids leaning against
the tree. Another idea took shape in her mind, and she
fumbled in her reticule for her handkerchief.

She kicked Polly, who was sitting opposite her, and the
maid yelped in terror.

"What is it, Polly?" she asked anxiously. "Do you feel
sick? Please, Stephen, open this window a fraction, else
I'm afraid Polly will be ill." She slid over to sit next to her.

Stephen hesitated.

"For heaven's sake, hurry. No one from the house will
notice if you open this one," she said, indicating the one
window that faced the gardens. She dug Polly in the ribs,
and the girl cried out again.

Stephen quickly pulled the window down six inches.
"This will have to suffice," he said. "But, I'm warning you,
Roberta, don't do anything that will force me to use this
pistol."

Polly saw the gun pointed at her, and with a final gurgle
of terror, she fainted away.

At that moment the carriage door nearest the house swung
open, and the comte climbed in. As he took his seat, Roberta
stood up and quickly pushed her handkerchief out of the
window.

"Sit down, Mademoiselle Rushforth," the comte said.
"We have a long way to go, and you will be more comfortable seated."

Roberta did as he suggested but refused to acknowledge
his presence. She kept her eyes firmly on the window,
craning her neck to keep Davids in sight as the coach moved
off. Just as they rounded the bend in the road, she saw the
shadowy form of Davids cross the street and stoop to retrieve
her handkerchief.

Her despair of a few moments ago diminished slightly,
and she turned to face the comte with calmness.

"I trust I have not put you to too much inconvenience,
Mademoiselle Rushforth," the comte said smoothly. "And
I see we have the pleasure of your maid's company in place

of the redoubtable Mrs. Ashley. Will you not introduce us?"

"I have nothing to say to you, monsieur," Roberta responded haughtily, "except that I think you are the most despicable man it has been my misfortune to meet."

He laughed and reached out to touch her, then laughed again when he felt her shudder. "Really, mademoiselle? I feel confident you will change your mind when we reach France. Especially when Sir Nicholas will no longer be able to help you and I am the only friend you have."

Roberta shook her head, stubbornly refusing to let his taunting frighten her. She would endure anything rather than give him the satisfaction of seeing her concern.

"If she thinks by ignoring me, Stephen," the comte continued genially, "I will tire of her company, she will find she is mistaken. Did you not tell her that I always get what I want?"

"I did, monsieur. She will come around in time, I'm sure."

Roberta bit hard on her lower lip to prevent herself from uttering the words of protest that sprang to her mind, and pulled her arm away from the comte's grasp. Sir Nicholas might not love her, but he wouldn't act in the cowardly fashion Stephen had just suggested. And as she pondered Stephen's words, she felt a sudden rush of excitement. He had said, 'will refuse'! Surely that would indicate that Sir Nicholas was still alive. And if he was still alive, there was yet hope that Davids would be of some help once they reached Richmond.

Feeling somewhat comforted by her thoughts, Roberta drew her cloak about her and closed her eyes.

"It would appear that mademoiselle is tired, Stephen," the comte said. "Perhaps we should let her rest, for once we leave Richmond, there will be little opportunity to sleep."

Roberta sighed in relief. Her ruse to silence the men had worked, and she felt she had gained a little victory.

They sped through the night. Through half-closed eyes, Roberta saw Polly stir. For a moment, she was afraid the girl would draw attention to herself and thus be subjected to further taunts from the comte. But Polly, after opening her eyes to look about her, closed them firmly again.

The problem of what to do with Polly once they had reached Richmond was still weighing heavily on Roberta's mind when Stephen's voice broke the silence.

"How much further?" he inquired of the comte.

"We'll be there in a few minutes," he responded. "I'll leave Jacques in charge of the two ladies. You and I will have enough to do in taking care of Sir Nicholas."

"I told Jacques to conceal the coach in the copse at the end of the lane," Stephen said. "I thought it best not to herald our arrival by driving up to the house. There is a side entrance we can use."

"Good," the comte said with a grunt. The coach came to a halt. "Get down, Stephen, and ask Jacques to join me."

Roberta closed her eyes tightly, feigning sleep, but the awkward swaying of the carriage indicated that Stephen had gone and the coachman had entered.

"Jacques," the comte murmured softly, "don't let these two ladies out of the carriage. We'll be back anon. I don't think they will attempt to escape, but have your pistol ready just in case."

Jacques didn't respond, but Roberta imagined him nodding. Then the carriage swayed once more, and she knew that the comte had departed. She opened her eyes, and immediately Jacques leveled his pistol at her.

"What is going to happen to me?" she asked. When he shrugged uncomprehendingly, she repeated the question in French.

"Be quiet," he snapped.

"Do you mind if I lower the window a little more?" she asked in subdued tones. "I'm feeling a trifle faint."

Jacques nodded his approval.

She moved slowly, for her legs were cramped from having sat too long. She pushed the window down and inhaled the fresh air greedily. As she did so, she peered through the trees and saw a forbidding-looking house, bathed in moonlight. Its square, ugly structure threw black shadows on the surrounding area. She wondered if the coachman would shoot her in the back if she dared make a dash for it, and her fingers closed about the handle on the door. It moved beneath her touch, and the door flew open. She grabbed wildly for any kind of support, but it was in vain. She tumbled down to the ground, and a searing pain shot up her leg. She bit fiercely on her lower lip to prevent herself from crying out, and suddenly her mouth was filled with her own blood.

"Get up slowly, mademoiselle," Jacques ordered brusquely. He had jumped down after her and was now standing over her.

"I don't think I can manage," she gasped as she struggled to stand.

He reached down and grasped her hand. As he did so, Roberta saw the shadowy figure of another man behind him, his right arm raised, and his hand clutching a thick stick.

She screamed and fainted.

chapter 19

AFTER DAVIDS HAD rendered the coachman senseless, he bound the man's arms with his muffler and used a handkerchief to gag him. Then he dragged him to some nearby bushes and rolled him under them.

"That should suffice for the time being," he muttered, and hurried over to Roberta, whom he picked up with ease and placed gently on the coach floor.

"Polly, are you there?" he inquired softly. "Are you all right?"

"Dickie, is that really you?" Polly shrieked, and, without any thought for her own safety, she threw herself into his waiting arms. She started to sob hysterically, and Davids quickly covered her mouth with his.

"Hush, hush, my dearest," he whispered at length. "We haven't much time."

"Oh, Dickie!" she mumbled as she tried to control her sobs. "If only I had known you were following us. I've been so frightened. And Miss Roberta was so brave. How did you know I was here? Oh, Dickie! I'm ever so glad to see you." Her words tumbled out in a rush.

"Not half as glad as I am to see you, love," Davids interposed quickly when she paused for breath. "Now, take a deep breath to steady your nerves while I decide what's to be done. We none of us expected the complication that you and Miss Rushforth would be in the carriage with the comte. Although, now that I think on it, I blame myself entirely for not being suspicious when Lord Bromley's footman told me that you and Miss Rushforth had gone to visit Lady Anita. We'd best get to Sir Nicholas and let him know his plan has gone awry."

"It's too late," Polly gasped. "That awful man and Mr. Davenport have already gone to the house. They said something about Lord Bromley and Sir Nicholas walking into a trap."

Davids swore softly under his breath. "Then we have even less time than I thought." He lowered Polly to her feet and gave her a reassuring squeeze. "You'll have to walk, love, while I carry Miss Rushforth. Hold on to my coattails if you get nervous."

Polly nodded and watched as he gathered Roberta into his arms.

"We'll circle round to the stables, kitten," Davids murmured as they started walking, "and see if Sir Nicholas is there. I was supposed to meet him there later tonight if everything went according to plan. Mayhap we can catch him before it's too late."

Polly, emboldened by his words of endearment, kept close to his side, and they continued to walk in silence.

They had almost attained the stables when they were arrested by the sound of an approaching carriage. Davids lengthened his stride and entered the stables just as the carriage pulled into the driveway.

Sir Nicholas appeared immediately. "What on earth are you doing here so soon, Davids—" he began, breaking off when he recognized Roberta. He stepped over and relieved Davids of his burden. "What, in heaven's name, is the meaning of this? Is she badly injured?" he asked urgently.

He looked down at Roberta tenderly and tightened his grip as she stirred slightly. Her pallor gave him cause for concern.

"It's just her ankle, I think, Sir Nicholas. She fainted before I could ask her any questions."

"Was she alone?"

Davids shook his head. "Polly was with her, and the comte's coachman. I left him under some bushes."

"Then who has just arrived?" Sir Nicholas queried.

"That must be Jenkins, sir. You see, with Miss Rushforth and Polly's being in the comte's carriage, we thought it best not to stop him as planned."

"What on earth were they doing in the comte's carriage?" Sir Nicholas asked, and then shook his head. "On second thought, you can tell me later. What's more important at the moment is the whereabouts of the comte."

"Polly thinks both he and Mr. Davenport have gone into the house."

"In that case, I think I'll follow them," Sir Nicholas said tersely. "You take Polly back to the coachman in case he comes to, and on your way, inform Jenkins to stay outside until he hears from me."

"Yes, Sir Nicholas," Davids responded, and slipped back outside, taking Polly with him.

Sir Nicholas, carrying Roberta, followed moments later. He walked boldly across the front lawns and entered the house by the main door.

Lord Bromley hurried out of one of the side rooms and joined him. I think I just heard a carriage," he said, and then broke off as he saw Roberta. "It can't be!" he exclaimed. "What has happened?"

"I don't know, John," Sir Nicholas answered. "Davids found her outside with one of the comte's men."

"The fiend!" Lord Bromley shouted. "If he has harmed her in any way, he'll suffer for it!"

Sir Nicholas gave a short laugh. "He'll pay for it with his life, John. Both he and Davenport are somewhere inside the house. We had best wait for them in here."

He strode into the dimly lit gaming room and placed Roberta gently on a couch. Kneeling beside her he took one of her hands and massaged it tenderly. She looked so frail and lifeless, and his concern for her deepened. He felt powerless to resist the urge to kiss her, and, without pausing to consider Lord Bromley's presence, he brushed his lips against her cheek. She stirred, and this time she opened her eyes. She touched her cheek where he had kissed her and stared at him in breathless wonder. There was so much she wanted to say, but she seemed to have no control over her thoughts. She struggled to sit up, but Sir Nicholas held her down firmly.

"Stay where you are, my darling," he whispered tenderly. "You had a nasty fall."

She reached out and caressed his face, tracing a line from his forehead to his mouth. It was, she realized, something she had long wanted to do.

He kissed her again, this time on her eyelids, and she trembled in ecstasy.

"Oh, Nicholas, Nicholas, you're alive!" she cried. "I was certain I would be too late."

Lord Bromley hurried to her side and gripped her other hand.

"Roberta, tell us what happened," Sir Nicholas said, ignoring Lord Bromley. "It's important we know."

"I think I can answer that question for you, Sir Nicholas. Mademoiselle Rushforth has foolishly tried to escape from me."

Sir Nicholas stiffened at the sound of the comte's voice and reached inside his jacket for his pistol.

Lord Bromley quickly put a restraining hand on his arm. "Be calm, Nicholas, my boy," he growled. "The comte is holding Davids."

Sir Nicholas rose slowly to his feet. "It would appear Miss Rushforth has succeeded, Monsieur le Comte," he bluffed in a calm voice. "It must irk you to know that a woman has outwitted you." He swung round and swore softly when he saw that the comte was holding a gun to David's head. Something had gone dreadfully wrong with his carefully laid plans.

"Move away from the couch," the comte ordered brusquely. "And don't make any sudden moves, else this man of yours, Sir Nicholas, dies."

Both Lord Bromley and Sir Nicholas complied, and the comte quickly propelled Davids to the couch. He positioned himself so that Roberta lay between himself and the two men. Then, without warning, he twisted Davids's arm back with a savage jerk.

"Now, gentlemen," the comte said, "if you would be good enough to throw down any weapons you happen to have, I think I can accomplish my goal without bloodshed."

Sir Nicholas shrugged in resignation. While Roberta was in such a vulnerable position and the whereabouts of Stephen and Polly unknown, he dared not disobey. He pulled out one of a pair of small dueling pistols he was carrying, from his jacket. He let it rest in his hand for a moment before leaning over to place it on a small low table close to Roberta's right hand.

Sir Nicholas stepped back quickly to Lord Bromley's
side.

"Lord Bromley, where are your weapons?" the comte
asked.

"I'm not armed. I don't hold with violence."

"For your niece's sake, I hope you're not lying. What
have you done with the three men I left here to greet you,
Sir Nicholas? Are they still alive?"

"Don't think to use them to help you escape," Sir Nicholas answered. "They are in the cellars, and, with the amount
of drugged brandy they have consumed, I doubt they will
wake before morning."

"And Veronique?"

"Who?"

"Don't play me for a fool," the comte snarled. "Order
her to come in here, before I lose my temper."

Sir Nicholas shrugged again and sauntered to the door.
"She will be of little help to you now," he said. The comte
frowned.

"Veronique!" Sir Nicholas shouted. "You can come
down." He leaned casually against the door post.

When Veronique appeared, her eyes were wide with fear,
and Sir Nicholas knew that she would be of little help to
him either. That left Lacey and Jenkins.

"The young man I asked you to entertain, Veronique,
is he still asleep upstairs?" the comte asked sharply.

Veronique glanced nervously at Sir Nicholas before re-
sponding. "I don't know where he is. I—I think that man,"
she said, pointing to Lord Bromley, "had him taken away.
I was powerless to stop him."

"Was he still drugged?" the comte asked.

Veronique shrugged helplessly. "I—I suppose . . ."

"She doesn't have the presence of mind of Miss Rushforth," Sir Nicholas interposed swiftly even as the comte
was nodding in satisfaction at Veronique's reply. "I'm surprised you didn't instruct the poor girl in the basics of self-
defense," he added, afraid that if Veronique was allowed
to continue, she would confess that she hadn't, in fact,
drugged Sir Lacey and that he was at this very moment
somewhere in the house.

"Please, Monsieur le Comte," Veronique cried. "I've

done nothing wrong. I'll do anything to help you just so long as you let me go. I've got my brother to think of. There's only me to look after him."

The comte laughed. "You see, my fine Englishman. It matters not that my women aren't savages. As long as one discovers where they are most vulnerable, they're easily controlled. Veronique, take the cords holding the curtains, and tie the hands of the two gentlemen behind their backs."

"And you'll let me go?"

"Don't argue, you little fool. Do as I say."

Veronique ran to the curtains and pulled at the cords until they fell away. In her haste to be gone, she tied Lord Bromley hurriedly and fled.

"How far do you think you'll get before you're stopped?" Sir Nicholas asked, trying to divert the comte's attention.

"With Mademoiselle Rushforth in our party, I think I can persuade your men to let us proceed. If I am stopped, I shall kill her without compunction," he snapped.

Lord Bromley's voice exploded across the room. "You're mad!" he shouted. "Quite, quite mad. Kill me, if need be, but leave my niece alone."

"Aren't you being a trifle overdramatic, monsieur?" Sir Nicholas drawled in an effort to give Lord Bromley time to recover. "She will not be of much use to you if you carry out your threat."

"She will pay eventually for what she has done," the comte responded angrily. "That any of you were stupid enough to think I would be fooled for long about mademoiselle having a father is beyond my comprehension. And as for you, Sir Nicholas, it is going to be my pleasure to deal with you personally. Your charade of calling my colleague out on the pretext of settling an affair of the heart is laughable. You didn't seriously believe that Stephen was taken in, I hope."

"Then the man's a fool and a coward to have agreed," Sir Nicholas responded coldly.

"He agreed to your absurd suggestion of meeting at dawn tomorrow, knowing that he would no longer be in England, Sir Nicholas. He was simply obeying my orders."

Roberta looked across at her uncle and attempted a smile. No matter what the outcome of the drama now being enacted, she would always draw comfort from the knowledge that Sir Nicholas was prepared to fight for her honor.

"And where is this fine specimen of an English gentleman now?" Sir Nicholas asked. "Holding poor Polly? Now that I consider it a moment, a frightened serving wench is about all I would entrust him to guard." There was a biting sarcasm to his voice which he hoped Davids would disregard. But it was the only way he knew to goad the comte into telling him who else Stephen was holding. It was essential that he knew whether Jenkins was free, before he made his move.

"Then it's quite obvious you don't know him as well as I," the comte retorted. "He is a fine man, and has performed well. And for your information, Sir Nicholas, he managed to subdue your man, Jenkins, without any difficulty at all."

"Leaving you the more difficult task of taking Davids and Polly," Sir Nicholas responded. "It doesn't surprise me in the least that he chose to tackle the easier target." His light bantering tone hid the deep concern he felt for Jenkins, for he knew his servant would not have surrendered without a fight. "I hope he, at least, had the decency to take care of any wound he might have inflicted on Jenkins."

"Polly's looking after him, Sir Nicholas," Davids said. "She knows what to do for a cut."

"So the brave young man used his rapier, did he?" Sir Nicholas asked, endeavoring to get a clearer picture of the scene outside.

"Enough of your idle chatter," the comte snapped impatiently. With an angry gesture, he flung Davids away from him and in a thick voice ordered him to pick up Roberta. "Carry her to the coach in the driveway," he ordered. "Mr. Davenport is waiting for you there."

Davids moved with deliberate slowness and for a few seconds managed to conceal Roberta from the comte's view.

Sir Nicholas, watching through narrowed eyes, silently applauded when he saw Roberta reach out and take the gun from the table.

"Be careful you don't drop her, Davids," he drawled. "She has injured her ankle."

Davids grinned conspiratorially at Sir Nicholas. "I'll treat her like she's a piece of the finest crystal," he said. He leaned over and lifted her up. Under the pretense of making her comfortable in his arms, he took the gun.

The comte poked his gun into the small of Davids's back and ordered him to lead the way. "You will follow, Sir Nicholas, when I nod, and you, Lord Bromley, will come with me."

Davids started for the door, and as he passed Sir Nicholas, Roberta murmured, "Is there anything I can do to help?"

"Davids will drop you once you're outside. Roll away and don't move until I come for you," he whispered.

Roberta craned her neck for one last look at Sir Nicholas, marveling at his coolness.

"What is going to happen?" she whispered. "How will my uncle and Sir Nicholas defend themselves with their arms tied behind their backs?"

"The element of surprise will be on our side," Davids responded, "for I happened to notice that Lord Bromley loosened his bonds a few minutes ago." With an awkward motion, he opened the front door, and a blast of cold air made Roberta shiver. "Can you see Sir Nicholas over my shoulder yet?" he asked as he paused at the head of the stone steps.

"He's just coming out of the room now. And there's the comte and my uncle."

Davids grunted. "When I get to the bottom of these steps, I'm going to turn to the right and drop you. There is a lavender bush a few yards farther along. Head for that. I'll cut back to my left and proceed as if I'm still holding you."

Roberta's heart beat faster as Davids descended. The last glimpse she had of Sir Nicholas was of him turning to make some comment to the comte. Even as Davids dropped her and she rolled toward the bush, she wondered what Sir Nicholas had thought to say to delay the comte's progress to the door.

She had barely gained the cover of the bush when she felt a hand cover her mouth. She screamed, but no sound came. She struggled furiously, but her strength was no match against the man holding her. She sagged against him as tears of frustration gathered in her eyes.

"Miss Rushforth, are you all right?"

"Sir Lacey!" she exclaimed. "Where on earth have you been?"

Sir Lacey grinned. "Waiting for you to leave the house. Where did Davids go?"

"To the carriage. He's armed, though I have no idea what he intends to do."

Sir Lacey swore softly and stood up. "Davenport will get him, too," he murmured. "Stay here," he added, and before she could ask what he meant, he had melted into the shadows.

She watched in fearful fascination as Sir Nicholas appeared on the top step, the comte and Lord Bromley joining him moments later. They seemed to be arguing; the silhouetted scene had an eerie quality about it. Then she saw Lord Bromley drop the cords that bound his hands, and with a speed that belied his age, he pushed the comte down the steps.

The comte landed awkwardly, and the gun he was holding fell from his grasp and slid across the lawn toward her. By the time the comte had risen to his feet, Sir Nicholas, his hands now free, was at his side. Lord Bromley had disappeared.

Sir Nicholas quickly seized the comte by the arm and, using the cord that had so recently bound his own hands, tied the comte's hands behind his back. "You are surrounded, Monsieur le Comte," he said. "I wouldn't do anything foolish." Then: "Lacey, are you there?" he shouted over his shoulder. Sir Lacey emerged from the inky darkness. "Take him inside," Sir Nicholas commanded, "while I deal with Davenport."

"He fled in your carriage a few moments ago, as Davids and I were helping Jenkins to his feet," Sir Lacey replied. "I didn't give chase, for Davids assured me that Lord Bromley's men will stop him."

Sir Nicholas turned to the comte and laughed. "So much for your loyal colleague," he said. "But worry not, monsieur. You will have plenty of time in which to tell him just what you think of his cowardly behavior when you both stand trial for treason."

The comte's shoulder's slumped in defeat, and Roberta watched as Sir Lacey led him away. When she looked back to where Sir Nicholas had been standing, he was no longer there. She sat up and glanced about anxiously. When she couldn't see anyone, her anxiety increased, and she rolled out from under the bush.

The noise of a breaking twig, followed by a mild oath, caused her to turn. Sir Nicholas was a foot away, on his hands and knees, peering into the bush. If she stretched out a hand, she could have touched him.

Unable to control her mirth at his undignified position, she giggled. Suddenly she felt his arms about her, and tears of joy spilled down her cheeks.

"There, there, my darling girl," he murmured. "It's all over now. You're quite safe."

"Oh, my precious Nicholas!" she cried. "I know, I know. My tears are ones of happiness at being here with you."

He looked at her strangely for a moment and then crushed her to him. "I never thought to hear you say that, my love. I worried that after all the suffering I had caused you, you would never want to see me again."

"And until tonight I thought you didn't want to see *me* again," she confided shyly.

"Does this mean, Miss Rushforth, that you are prepared to change your mind and accept my proposal after all?" he asked in a voice that quivered with emotion.

She pushed him away slightly, for she still hadn't heard the words she most wanted to hear. "Is this declaration prompted by pity?" she asked wickedly.

"You minx," he responded. "You must know that this one comes from my heart. I love you, my darling. I love you to distraction."

His lips found hers, and he kissed her passionately. As she surrendered to his embrace, a sigh of pure contentment escaped her.

The sound of approaching footsteps caused them to pull apart. Sir Nicholas rose to his feet and helped Roberta to hers. She leaned against him for support.

"Goddammit! Jenkins, Davids, have neither of you got a flint? I can't see anyone here." Lord Bromley's voice broke angrily through the silence.

"I believe there are some in the house, John," Sir Nicholas answered with a laugh. "Who are you looking for?"

"The comte, for a start."

"He's in the house," Sir Nicholas said, "with his hands tied firmly behind his back."

"And Roberta, where is she? Davids has had the devil's own time searching for her, because the confounded moon fled behind some clouds. For all we know, she is lying somewhere, seriously injured."

"I'm here, Uncle," Roberta said gaily.

"Where?" Lord Bromley demanded.

"At my side, where she belongs," Sir Nicholas answered as he turned to gather her into his arms.

Lord Bromley hurried over to them just as Sir Lacey appeared with a lighted lamp. They stopped short when they saw the radiant expression on Roberta's face.

"Do I offer you my congratulations now, Nicholas?" he asked.

"She hasn't accepted my proposal yet, but I am confident she will. I anticipate our wedding will take place in the very near future." .

Roberta gazed up at Sir Nicholas adoringly. "Would tomorrow be soon enough?" she inquired breathlessly, and kissed him gently on his cheek. Then, overcome with emotion, she buried her face in his jacket.

Davids, who had been following close behind, halted when he heard this. With a whoop of joy that took everyone by surprise, the threw his tricorn into the air and turned to embrace Polly.

QUESTIONNAIRE

1. How many romances do you *read* each month? _____

2. How many of these do you *buy* each month? _____

3. Do you read primarily
   - ☐ novels in romance lines like SECOND CHANCE AT LOVE
   - ☐ historical romances
   - ☐ bestselling contemporary romances
   - ☐ other _____

4. Were the love scenes in this novel (this is book # _____)
   - ☐ too explicit
   - ☐ not explicit enough
   - ☐ tastefully handled

5. On what basis do you make your decision to buy a romance?
   - ☐ friend's recommendation
   - ☐ bookseller's recommendation
   - ☐ art on the front cover
   - ☐ description of the plot on the back cover
   - ☐ author
   - ☐ other _____

6. Where did you buy this book?
   - ☐ chain store (drug, department, etc.)
   - ☐ bookstore
   - ☐ supermarket
   - ☐ other _____

7. Mind telling your age?
   - ☐ under 18
   - ☐ 18 to 30
   - ☐ 31 to 45
   - ☐ over 45

8. How many SECOND CHANCE AT LOVE novels have you read?
   - ☐ this is the first
   - ☐ some (give number, please _____)

9. How do you rate SECOND CHANCE AT LOVE vs. competing lines?
   - ☐ poor
   - ☐ fair
   - ☐ good
   - ☐ excellent

10. Check here if you would like to
    - ☐ receive the SECOND CHANCE AT LOVE Newsletter

· ·

Fill-in your name and address below:

name:_____

street address:_____

city_____ state_____ zip_____

Please share your other ideas about romances with us on an additional sheet and attach it securely to this questionnaire.

PLEASE RETURN THIS QUESTIONNAIRE TO:
SECOND CHANCE AT LOVE, THE BERKLEY/JOVE PUBLISHING GROUP
200 Madison Avenue, New York, New York 10016